The
SAND
DOG

SARAH LEAN

HarperCollins *Children's Books*

First published in Great Britain by
HarperCollins *Children's Books* in 2018
HarperCollins *Children's Books* is a division of HarperCollins*Publishers* Ltd,
HarperCollins Publishers
1 London Bridge Street
London SE1 9GF

The HarperCollins website address is:
www.harpercollins.co.uk
1

ISBN 978-0-00-816581-9

Typeset in 12.5pt Goudy by Palimpsest Book Production Ltd,
Falkirk, Stirlingshire
Printed and bound in England by CPI Group (UK) Ltd, Croydon CR0 4YY

For my nephew Seb (lead guitar – Chapman's Farm, vintage, Pops) Granville

1

I NEVER THOUGHT GRANDFATHER WOULD COME back on an ordinary day like a Monday or a Tuesday. He'd come on the kind of day when the rising sun is pouring its colours on the sea because there's not enough room for all its glory in the sky. Grandfather was like that kind of special day to me too. He was a fisherman, and from watching the drift of deep-water seaweed he could land a net of fish full to bursting. He knew the journey of a past storm by what swept up on the beach, and could tell a thousand stories of extraordinary creatures from the deep. He said that the ocean had a long story to tell about all of us, full of signs of things that have happened and signs of things that are to come. I always knew he'd come back across the sea, triumphing over a few monsters on the way, but I was still waiting after two years for that special day to arrive.

I live on a small island in the Mediterranean. My home used to be with Grandfather in a little fisherman's cottage but now I'm in a flat with Uncle above his restaurant at the back of the beach. My open bedroom window is like an ear to the sounds of the water, and it was one Friday night that I heard the rhythm of the tide change.

In my underpants, I went downstairs and walked

across the beach to look out over the waves. The sea was black as simmering tar, and the moon reflected like broken glass on the restless waves. At the far end of the beach on the shallow rocks that divided the beach from the cove further along, a turtle was struggling hard to climb out of the water. Her shell was patterned like the crazy paving of our narrow streets, and I wondered what it felt like to carry her home on her back.

The turtle was clumsy on the rocks without the support of the water, and tumbled on her back to the sandy cove. I ran over. Turtles aren't good on land anyway, but her front flipper was caught in some fishing line round her neck like a sling, making it hard for her to move at all. I recognised the chip in her shell from when she'd been to our island two years ago. I wondered if she remembered me, because she didn't seem afraid when I rolled her over. She was heavy, and as big as a shield, but I was strong and cut her free from the line. She lumbered off, digging grooves in the sand with her flippers, leaving a rippled pattern beside my footprints. Slowly she made her way to the back of the cove where she dug a cool hole, laid her eggs and buried them deep in the dark, just as she had before. I stayed with her until she was ready to go back to the sea, as the sun rose pink and gold behind a thin bank of cloud at dawn.

Grandfather had taught me that the sea could tell me a story. I needed three signs to let me know that he was coming home. The turtle had been the same one I'd seen the day before he left. Could that be the first sign?

I swam and dived with the turtle in the growing day, in the place where she was at ease, where I felt at home too, until I heard Uncle shouting from the rocks, 'Azi! Get out of the sea! It's almost eight o'clock!'

I surfed in with a wave and followed Uncle up to the restaurant where he was already laying tables ready for the early tourists.

'Hurry up, or you'll be late,' he said. 'And don't forget your jobs after school!' he yelled, as I leaped up the stairs to the flat, two at a time, to get dressed.

I pulled on a T-shirt and flip-flops and I ran, feet flapping, all the way to school, my wet under-pants seeping through my shorts. It was already hot and I hoped they'd dry out before I got there. I'd got used to people calling me names like sea boy and water boy, saying the sea had weed on me, but I didn't care today. It was the last day of term, a special and good day to feel that Grandfather was coming home at last. Three whole months of holiday lay ahead of us – enough time for Grandfather to see the turtle eggs hatch with me.

After school finished, Dimi, Chris and three other children asked me to play basketball with them.

'Come on, just this once, Azi,' Chris said. 'We need enough players for two teams.'

I shrugged. 'I'm going to the beach. I want to swim.'

'You're always going to the beach,' Dimi moaned. 'You can go anytime.'

We'd been stuck like this for a while now – them asking me to play basketball, me asking them to come swimming – none of us wanting to do what the other wanted. The last couple of years as we'd been growing up, we had grown apart.

'You're a weird creature from the sea, Azi!' Chris

shouted. 'And you don't even belong here!' He slammed down the ball as I ran, trying not to listen to what he had said and to what people always told me, my flip-flops slapping on the tarmac that had gone sticky in the heat.

I swam, looking for the turtle, but she had gone, so I went to Uncle's restaurant to talk to him about it. The restaurant was busy, the tables on the deck almost full of customers, white tablecloths swaying under the shade of the vines overhead.

In the kitchen, Uncle's face was red and sweaty from the ovens and the scorching day.

'The turtle came back,' I said. 'Do you remember the one that came the day before Grandfather left?'

Uncle frowned but didn't answer. He was trying to take an order ticket from Maria the waitress, but she held on to it, her other hand on her hip, nodding her head towards me, waiting for Uncle to answer me first.

'It must be a sign that he's coming home. Have you heard from him?' I said.

'Two calamari!' Uncle yelled to the other staff bustling and sweating around him as he tried to read the ticket between Maria's fingers.

'Azi is trying to speak to you,' Maria said.

'Two Greek salads!' Uncle yelled, snapping the ticket from Maria. She clicked her tongue on her teeth because he was yelling, even though he didn't need to, but she wasn't ever bothered by his loud presence and the fact that he was the boss. 'I don't know anything about turtles,' Uncle said more quietly and turned away from me to toss fish in a frying pan.

'What's the turtle got to do with Grandfather, Azi?' Maria said, filling in for Uncle.

'Grandfather taught me to read the signs from the sea,' I explained. 'Things that wash up on the sand can tell you a kind of story.'

Maria raised her eyebrows. 'Is the turtle the same kind of sign as those big seashells you found on the beach? Or those waves breaking out like seahorses, and all the other signs you keep telling me about?'

I'd said the same kind of thing before, but this time it was different. This time I was sure it meant Grandfather was coming back. 'Grandfather told me turtles are messengers,' I said, hoping she'd understand.

At that moment, Uncle yelled across the kitchen. 'How many times have I told you all of Grandfather's talk was nonsense? And unless you're bringing me a turtle to make soup, Azi, out of my kitchen and go get me some more customers!'

Although I was used to Uncle yelling a lot of the time over pots and pans (and I knew he didn't really mean that he'd cook the turtle), you could hear the uncomfortable silence among the rest of the staff behind all the clanking and sizzling and chopping. Maria shook her head at Uncle, pursing her lips.

It wasn't the right time to talk to Uncle. The restaurant was quite full, but not as full as Uncle would have liked it, and that made him crabby. He relied on having lots of customers in the summer to keep the bills paid throughout the quiet winter. I collected the flyers that I usually handed out to people who came off the ferries at the quay and was about to leave when Maria called after me, her foot holding the swinging door open.

'Uncle yells at everyone, you know that, don't you?' she said. 'It's just a lot of hot air.'

'Grandfather used to say that if all of Uncle's yelling

didn't come out, it would boil and boil up inside him and then one day he'd go *kaboom*!' I said.

'Wouldn't be good for business if Uncle went *kaboom*, hey, Azi?' Maria laughed. 'Grandfather made sense to you, didn't he?'

I nodded. 'We're two of a kind, me and him. Two creatures from the sea.'

'And what's the message the turtle has brought you?' she said.

'People send messages to say they're coming, don't they?'

Maria smiled. 'Yes, they usually do.' She reached out and tugged at the end of my hair lying on my shoulders. 'When are you going to let me cut your hair?'

'When Grandfather comes back,' I said, running off.

* * *

At the quay, I called out to the tourists as they stepped off the ferries that brought them from the other islands.

'Come to Uncle's restaurant on the beach! Fresh fish. Hot chips and ketchup. Cold beer,' I told them, and handed out flyers, sticking some in the side pockets of suitcases as they were wheeled past. But most of the time I was checking to see if an old man in a blue cap would appear. When the ferries were finally emptied Grandfather hadn't come, so I headed off, not really sure when to expect him.

I went back to the cove and staked a fence made of driftwood sticks and chicken wire round the area where the turtle eggs were hidden. I stripped down to my shorts and swam, and from out in the water looked back to the land to see what the turtle must have seen when she'd found her way to the same nesting place. Except for that one time two years ago, we'd not had any other turtles nesting on our island before. Surely it couldn't just be a coincidence that the turtle had come back now.

Uncle's restaurant was only thirty running steps from the edge of the sea, but neither he nor Maria knew the sea like Grandfather and I did. I might have got it wrong before, but this time I was sure Grandfather was coming. The sea knew this story and it was telling me so.

2

THE SEA TAKES ITS OWN TIME TO TELL ITS STORY,
Grandfather once told me. It was here long before
we were and moved at its own pace and rhythm,
not ours. Uncle was too busy in the restaurant over
the weekend for me to talk to him again about
Grandfather but it didn't stop me thinking about
what had happened. Grandfather had left suddenly
to go to London, Uncle had said, to sort out an

old family problem. Grandfather hadn't been born here but neither had he been born in England, so I was sure he couldn't have family there. Why then had he never come back?

Uncle gave me lots of jobs to do over the weekend so it wasn't until Monday that I could go down to the beach again. I was out swimming at the cove when I saw a strange shape and shadow in the water and before long a blue door came floating in on the tide. Was this another sign? It wasn't the kind of thing you would normally find in the sea, but after the turtle had turned up I wasn't sure what to expect. I swam out to meet the door and climbed onboard. Although the paint on it was crackled and flaked away, it was the same colour blue as the one on Grandfather's cottage.

Grandfather had lost his fishing boat a while before he left, so it was nice to feel what it was like to have something solid to float on again. There was a hole in the door where the letter box used to be and I looked down through it at the shadow it made on the seabed. Then I dived under and looked up through the opening, blowing bubbles through the hole before climbing back up and lying on it, face down, like a wide surfboard. I paddled around for a while and then took it to shore. It was already so hot in June that you had to hop across the sand. I dug away to get to the cooler, damp sand underneath and then propped the door up with some rocks and sheltered in its shade, looking out across the water for the afternoon ferries. When I saw the first big white-and-yellow ferry in the distance I knew it was time to go down to the quay and hand out more flyers, and while I was waiting I noticed something on the rocks out of the corner of my eye.

I squinted in the light until I could just make out that it was a dog. How long must he have been sitting there? He was looking out to sea, his narrow nose up in the air in a kind of proud way. He sometimes glanced over at me but when I looked at him he would look away. Then when I looked away he would shuffle a bit closer. I guessed he must want some shade because the sand was oven-hot, so I moved over and soon he came and sat next to me under the shadow of the door. He was almost as tall as I was sitting down, long and lean, with wispy fur the colour of sand. He didn't do anything else but watch with his nose up while his ears drooped down. I wondered for a minute if he could be the third sign, but I decided he couldn't be because he hadn't actually come from the sea.

'What are *you* waiting for?' I said to him.

The dog's eyes twitched towards me for a moment, but looking out over the waves was all he seemed to want to do, and we sat there for a long time, just like that, until the yellow-and-white ferry turned into the quay.

'Gotta go,' I said to the dog. 'You can sit here, if you want, and keep watch for me.' The dog looked up. 'I'm waiting for another sign.'

At the quay, crowds of passengers disembarked.

'Come to Uncle's. Best restaurant on the beach,' I said. 'Calamari and chips. Ice-cold beer.'

I didn't think Grandfather would really come on a Monday but you never knew, so I was still keeping an eye out for a short white-haired old man with muscular shoulders and arms, because that door was definitely telling me something. Maybe it meant that a letter from Grandfather had come! I headed into the village.

At the post office hardly anyone was queuing. I looked through the doorway to see who was inside and nearly stopped myself from going in to speak to Mrs Halimeda because she was an impatient kind of person. But when everyone else had gone I took my chance, and stepped up to the counter.

Mrs Halimeda sighed. 'What is it this time, Azi?'

I folded one of the spare flyers, pushing it under the glass partition. 'I couldn't remember whether you'd seen Uncle's new menu,' I said.

She took it, unfolded it, and sighed again. 'It's exactly the same as the one you gave me last time you came in,' she said, pushing it back through the window.

I rolled and unrolled the paper in my fingers before finally saying what I was really there for. 'I wondered if there was a letter for me today?'

Mrs Halimeda narrowed her eyes. 'As I've told

you every week now for a very long time, if we did it would be delivered to your uncle's address like everything else is. And before you ask again, yes, we know where you live.'

I felt uncomfortable that I always seemed to annoy her but I wanted to be sure she hadn't missed anything.

'I found a door and I think it's a sign that something's been sent to me, you see,' I said.

Mrs Halimeda shook her head and looked over my shoulder as the queue began to grow behind me.

'What about a postcard?' I asked.

'No postcards,' she said, stern and as unmoved as a stone wall. 'Next!'

When I moved away I heard her saying 'Hopeless boy!' and the lady from the Turkish Baths replying, 'Well, you only have to look at who raised him.'

It burned inside and made me angry that they'd say something like that about me and Grandfather. But when people had called me names, or when they had looked at me as if I didn't belong here, Grandfather would say, 'They don't know you at all, not like I do.'

And they didn't know Grandfather like I did either.

When I went outside I found the dog from the cove was sitting beside the door. He put his nose in the air, looking away at first then looking back at me. Maybe his owner was in the post office.

Having no luck, I went back to the cove to check the turtle nest was safe from anybody disturbing it. As I was sitting there, digging away at my own hole in the sand with a stick to see how much work the mother turtle had to do to make her nest, a cool shadow fell across me, blocking the sun. It was the dog again, up on the rocks making shade for me. He climbed down and sat next to me again, looking out to sea.

'Do you like it here too?' I said.

He turned his head to look at me. His eyes were warm earth brown.

'Nobody can bother you here. There's just the whole wide sea . . . and us.'

The dog looked away when I didn't say any more.

I wrapped my arms round my shins, rubbing at the scar on my knee, and rested my chin there as I thought about Grandfather. Would he be coming on a ferry? Or would he have bought himself a new boat?

I remembered once when Grandfather and I had found broken wooden boxes scattered along the tideline of the cove. Then, a few days later, whole crates were washed up, and he said I had to wait and see what else came floating in. After about two weeks and loads of my guesses about what it might be (none of which were right), hundreds of pineapples had been washed up on the beach. The pineapples had come out of the boxes and must have fallen off a ship, but, because the boxes and pineapples were different shapes and weights and sizes, it had taken them different lengths of time to arrive. I'm not saying that Grandfather was a pineapple, and I definitely couldn't read the sea as well as he could, but it did mean that different things came at different times.

The dog sighed.

'Be patient, you've only been sitting here for one day,' I said. 'I've been waiting for two years for Grandfather to come home.'

We stayed like that again for a long, longing time.

3

THE NEXT MORNING, BEFORE UNCLE WAS UP, I stuffed some cold chicken and salad in pitta bread for breakfast and went down to the cove. The dog was already there, lying under the propped-up old door. His eyes and eyebrows twitched as he looked up at me but he didn't lift his head. I sat beside him and picked out the cucumber and tomatoes to eat them first. The dog sat up and was trying really hard not to look at me eating the rest.

'You must have got up early too so you're probably hungry,' I said, giving him a bit of chicken that he swallowed without chewing. It was nice having him beside me, even though he didn't say or do much; in fact, that was what I liked about him first of all. I liked that he'd sit there quietly with me looking out to sea. It was what Grandfather used to do.

'Stay there,' I told the dog. 'I'm going to get you something else.'

I ran back to Uncle's restaurant and found the old tin bucket out the back. Then I went to the kitchens and checked on the shelves in the fridge for plates covered in foil with leftovers from the restaurant. I piled food into the bucket, shut the fridge door and then found Uncle standing there.

'Who's all that food for?' he asked.

I wasn't sure what Uncle would say if he knew I was taking food for a dog. Sometimes there were strays around the restaurant – dogs that people brought on the ferries and left behind, sometimes on purpose, sometimes by mistake. Uncle said the strays put customers off, and the staff knew better than to feed them and chased them away. He probably wouldn't take kindly to the fact that I was encouraging one of them to hang about.

'It's all for me,' I said. 'I'm hungry.'

'Good,' he said, opening the fridge door to start preparing food. 'You need feeding up.'

It was a quiet moment without hot voices and burning ovens and the first time I'd had a chance to be with Uncle without him yelling for people to get a move on and take orders, clear tables or hurry up with those chips. This was my opportunity.

'Has Grandfather written to you to say which day he's coming back?' I asked.

Uncle had the same irritated look as Mrs Halimeda did when I kept asking the same question.

'No, he hasn't,' he said.

'Only I thought that if he's coming home soon, maybe I should go over to his cottage and put some food in the fridge, ready for when he comes back.'

Uncle put a plate down harder on the counter than he needed to and his voice grew like popcorn. I blinked as he told me, 'How many times have I said that you're not to go over there? You live here with me now, and that's that!'

I'd got used to Uncle's yelling and Mrs Halimeda's impatience and Chris and Dimi's mickey-taking but it was getting harder and harder to accept that this was how things had to be. Even though they all repeated the same things to me again and again, it wasn't what I wanted to hear. I belonged with Grandfather at his cottage, and while he wasn't here I felt like a bucketful of water that had been taken from the sea and left behind on the beach when the sun went down and everyone else had gone home. When you can't be with the person you need to be with all that you are left with is the longing to go back.

'I've taken care of you, and taught you good things, haven't I?' Uncle steadied himself and lowered his voice. 'You have everything you need here.'

'Yes, Uncle,' I said, which was what he wanted to hear.

He wrapped a chicken leg in a piece of foil and added it to my bucket. 'Eat it all – you're too skinny.'

I wasn't hungry after everything that Uncle had said, so when I went back to the cove I fed the dog with the food. 'You're the one that's too skinny,' I told him as he ate everything I gave him. He burped and then lay down on his side, exhausted from wolfing it all down in such a hurry, and he reminded me of Grandfather all over again.

Grandfather had a thousand tales to tell from his days on his fishing boat. Sometimes the stories would overlap or merge, one tale leading to another, while other times the stories would be familiar because he'd told a part of them before. Sometimes it was just because it included me and I'd already stored it in my memory. But the stories were never the same, never fully told, only narrow doorways into one whole story of our lives. The dog wasn't going to be able to tell me stories that made me feel like I belonged. He wouldn't know how to ride the storms that made waves as tall and hard as massive walls of stone, or have heard of giant squid that could wrap their tentacles round sailing boats and drag them to the depths, or about huge sea creatures with heads like hammers. I could sit and listen to Grandfather's stories for hours, my mouth wide open, daring it all to be true.

Without Grandfather, it was as if *my* history and the story I belonged in was missing the last chapter, the part when you finally get to hear how the monster is slayed.

Missing someone hurts all over. It's much worse than a jellyfish sting.

I looked at the dog. Maybe he'd like to hear about Grandfather instead.

'Once Grandfather saw the seabed split open and spit out fire from the centre of the Earth,' I told the dog.

He raised his head, his ears twitching when I threw my arms up and wide as if they were the Earth breaking open, shooting out fire with my hands, exploding, bubbling, up and up. The dog blinked.

'You ever seen such a thing?'

The dog's eyebrows twitched, and I nodded. 'The water boiled and the fish in Grandfather's nets were cooked before he hauled them in or even had a chance to get them to Uncle's kitchen, and he ate them, steaming, straight from the sea.'

The dog burped again and it made me laugh.

'It's true, dog. The boiling water cooked some seaweed too.'

I told him how the sea was full of things he couldn't imagine, that the sea was a story all by itself, the greatest story I had ever heard. 'Come on, dog, I'm going to show you something.'

31

I got up and went to the edge of the water with the bucket. It wasn't really the edge because the sea didn't have an edge as such because the sand was sometimes under the water and sometimes not. But, once upon a time, somebody had drawn a line on a map and said 'This is the edge of our country'.

A dark red piece of seaweed rolled to my feet, strands like an octopus's legs, waving with the rise and fall of the waves. I filled the tin bucket with seawater, poured in handfuls of sand, placed some small shells and waited for it all to settle. The dog looked in the bucket, sniffing at the wet, shiny weed I was holding, and then looked up at me, as if he was waiting for me to tell him something that might make sense of what we were looking at.

'This is what I wanted to show you,' I said. 'Grandfather says we have roots, like plants do, kind of like an invisible bit of us that is attached to where we belong, and part of us will always be joined there even when we leave.'

But there were plants in the sea that didn't have roots and drifted on the tides with nothing to hang on to. Grandfather had said that plants in the sea could only take root in the seabed where the water was shallow enough that the sunlight could still reach them.

The water in the bucket cleared and I pushed the end of the weed into the sand, finding a rock to hold it down on the bottom.

'The seaweed has to live here for a bit,' I said.

The strands unfurled, reaching towards the surface, and the dog and I stared into the mini aquarium I'd made. I used to find things to show Grandfather in the tin bucket. Back then, while I was diving in the water and he watched, he was the only one who really understood what it meant.

For the first time I touched the dog, stroking his head and neck, resting my hand on his shoulders. He seemed to like it, his eyes blinking slowly, as if he was feeling sleepy, or maybe remembering someone else's hand that made him feel nice.

'Even if we aren't in the place we think of as our home, we still all know where we belong,' I told him.

4

IN THE EARLY DAYS OF BEING ON THE FISHING boat with Grandfather he'd taught me to read the sea – if there was a flock of seabirds, a warm current and a kind of bubbling in the water, it meant a huge shoal of fish was feeding near the surface. Then Grandfather could throw out his nets and haul in a good catch. The lie of the rock, the deep shadows underneath and the way the fish emptied the space before gradually coming back (they have short memories and would forget quickly why they *weren't* feeding there), meant something else – it meant that in the dark, a moray eel with poisonous teeth would be waiting. From a distance you could poke under the rock with a long stick until the eel showed itself. Then you would know exactly what area to avoid to protect yourself.

I watched the sea to find the story I needed to hear. I wanted there to be a third sign that would tell me more about Grandfather coming home. But deep inside me I also had a feeling there was something else lurking – something lying, waiting in the dark, just like the moray eel under a rock. I needed to know what it was.

It was hot and sticky that night, the sky moody and heavy. I went to the restaurant kitchen while

Uncle was very busy to ask him again if he knew anything about Grandfather's return.

'Can't you see I'm busy?' Uncle yelled, but this time I stood my ground and didn't leave.

Maria stepped in again. 'Hold that,' she said, handing me the ladle from the mussel soup she'd been dishing into bowls. She pulled at Uncle's arm to get him to turn round. 'Azi needs an answer.'

The fired oven roared; plates ricocheted on tiled surfaces; glasses jangled on trays. Uncle told Maria that the people at table number five were waiting for their order, although we all knew he couldn't see from there. Hot plates whizzed past my ears, waiters and waitresses twirled around me and each other to get the orders out quickly, and to bring back dirty plates, as Uncle yelled at them to get a move on. I waited for an answer.

'Uncle, you know and I know that Grandfather

is coming back,' I said. In the dizzy tempest of the sizzling kitchen Uncle's arm touched a boiling-hot pan and he jumped away but I carried on. 'I only want to know *when*.'

'He's a drunk old fool and he's *not* coming back!' Uncle yelled. 'Not ever.'

Stunned, I dropped the metal ladle and it hit the floor, *clang-clanging* as it bounced. All of the movement and noise of the kitchen stopped, except for the fiery breath of the oven.

'Now get back to work,' Uncle said uncomfortably, and the bustle erupted again.

Maria swooped over, picked up the ladle and led me out to the stairs to the flat. 'Take no notice of Uncle. It's one of the busiest days ever and we're a bit pushed, that's all,' she said. 'He thinks the world of you, Azi.'

I wasn't going to ask Uncle about Grandfather

again. Now that Uncle had exploded and told me what he thought, it reminded me that I'd also been hiding my deepest secret in the dark. It was my fault that Grandfather had left.

The next day, when I went to the quay, I saw that the dog was following a little way behind me, head down, trotting slowly with stiff old legs. He lay in the shadow under a bench with his head on his paws but didn't close his eyes while all the passengers got off the ferries.

When everyone had gone to find B&Bs, shops, beaches and restaurants, all that was left was me, the dog and a small dark-red booklet that had been dropped on the quayside. I went over and picked it up. It was a British passport, and inside was a photograph of a girl called Beth Saunders who had been born in London.

Could this be the third sign from the sea? The girl that the passport belonged to was from exactly the same place that Uncle had said that Grandfather had gone – London. What could it mean? And then I knew what I had to do. I had to go and get him. I had to go to where he was staying and bring him back.

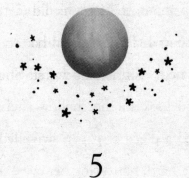

5

'THAT'S TWICE THIS WEEK YOU'VE BEEN IN here, Azi,' Mrs Halimeda said, irritated again on Thursday, looking at me like she always did, as if I smelled of rotting fish. 'Yes, I've seen Uncle's menu, and, no, I've still nothing for you.' She looked over my shoulder to see who was next.

'Can I have a passport?' I said.

She squinted and took ages to reply. 'What do you need a passport for?'

I knew not to tell Mrs Halimeda anything she could gossip about, so I mumbled something about a possible school trip in the future.

She frowned. 'You need a form.' She swivelled her chair to look in the shallow shelves behind her, selected a piece of paper, swivelled back and stared at me hard, narrowing her eyes. 'You'll have to give it to Uncle to fill out and sign.'

I assured her I would do that. 'Also, I found a passport.' I held up the one I'd found at the quay and she told me to take it to the lost-property office instead.

'Let that boy bother someone else for a change,' I heard her mutter to the next customer. It stung but I just kept thinking of Grandfather, of belonging with him again.

The dog was sitting outside the post office and watched with interest as I tucked the passport form inside my shorts and under my T-shirt.

'I've got to be with Grandfather, nobody else knows me like he does,' I said to him.

I didn't go to the lost-property office, though. I thought I might hang on to the passport in case it helped me to answer any questions on the form.

As I was going along the road I heard someone shout, 'Oi! Aqua boy!'

I turned to see Chris coming up the street with Dimi.

They came and stood by me. Chris was carrying his basketball. I was expecting them to ask me to play again, but they didn't this time.

'What are you doing?' Chris asked, bouncing his ball.

Dimi rolled his eyes, obviously knowing what my answer would be.

Grandfather and I had both liked it when nobody was there at the cove with us, and there was nothing but the sand and the sea. It had been a long time since anybody had been there with me.

'Do you want to see a turtle nest?' I said.

Chris said no first of all, but Dimi nudged him and said, 'Yeah, we might.'

'Show us,' Chris said.

We roamed along the shoreline where tourists speckled the sand with sunhats and towels, sunbeds and umbrellas, some paddling in the sea, their voices babbling in the distance. I told Chris and Dimi they wouldn't be able to see any turtles yet but I could show them the nest and we could keep watch over the summer. But all they wanted to do was push and shove, kicking at the sand, slamming the ball at each other's back. I saw the dog nearby, walking along stiffly, his head down.

'The nest is in the cove over the other side of the rocks,' I said, pointing in the direction of where the turtle had been. 'I've put a fence round it so nobody touches it. By the end of August the eggs will hatch.'

Chris and Dimi looked over to where I pointed but they were not interested any more and just ran off in the opposite direction when they saw some of the other boys over by the jet-ski school, laughing and shouting back at me, 'Forget it, turtle boy.'

I sighed. Who needed them anyway? The dog came over and sat down beside me at the cove. I didn't know why he kept following me around.

'You still lost your owner?' I said. 'Or maybe *you* want to come swimming with me instead.'

Grandfather was never fearful about me in the

water so I had never felt like I should be afraid, not even of the deep-sea monsters that he'd told tall tales about. All the stories of the battles between sea monsters and men were won in the end.

'What's out there?' I'd said, looking out to where the sea seemed endless.

'Nothing you need to be afraid of,' he'd say. 'There are no monsters that we can't overcome.'

As I thought about his words I waded out until the soft, cool water became my skin. It felt as if I disappeared when I dived under the surface; everything became a silent world of blue, including me. When I came up again the dog had waded into the sea after me. I showed the dog how not to be afraid of the water, staying near him, watching him, putting a hand under his belly when his feet left the ground. He was a natural. He made long doggy-paddle strokes, his nose up high, his body level in the water, graceful and calm, his stiffness all eased out. He seemed to like it too. As the dog circled me, I floated on my back with my arms out, held up by the water like driftwood, going wherever the sea took me. Before long, it pushed me back to the same shore.

The girl's passport wasn't much help in filling out the form. I wrote my name, address at Uncle's (I started to write Grandfather's but Mrs Halimeda would have something to say about that), and date of birth. I wrote in pencil first, trying to make my letters a bit slanted but neat, like an adult, before going over it slowly with a pen. Some of the questions were long and needed boxes ticking. At the end, there was a list of things I needed to send with it once it was signed, including a birth certificate and two photos.

People had told me for as long as I could

remember that I didn't belong on the island but when I had asked Grandfather why he had just teased me that it was because I had come from the sea. *You were born in the breaking waves, Azi, like a mermaid child.* He'd put his hand round the back of my head, pull me towards him and push the hair away to look behind my ears for gills. He'd beckon me to put my leg up on his knee, slipping off my flip-flop and rubbing the dust away.

'What are you looking for, Grandfather?' I'd say.

'Roots!' he would chuckle, and then laugh and laugh, feeling between my toes, then holding all my toes in his hand and peering at the bottom of my foot.

'Have I got roots, Grandfather?'

'Yes, Azi, yes!' he'd say, and I would crook up my knee and look at the dirt on the bottom, saying I couldn't see any.

'Roots are not *on* the sole, they're *in* your soul,' he'd tell me. He took the harsh words said by other people and made them vanish like salt dissolved in the sea because of what he thought of me.

That night, I was up in the flat while the restaurant was full, bubbling over with tourists, and Uncle seared and sizzled in the kitchen. I practised Uncle's signature over and over in pencil, rubbing it out if it didn't look right, trying again and again. All the rubbing made a rough place on the passport form, but eventually I thought it looked good enough.

I went through all the drawers and cupboards, and found the folder with all of our important documents, but there wasn't a birth certificate for me. Did Grandfather have it?

6

EARLY IN THE MORNING, BEFORE THE SUN HAD come up and while all the cool shadows were still merged into one, I left the restaurant with my pocket money and the girl's passport. The photo booth was outside the post office. I adjusted the stool, spinning round and round until it was the right height, straightened my T-shirt and pushed the hair away from my eyes, ready to take a picture.

I went to put a coin in but it dropped out of the slot and rolled out of the booth. When I bent down and reached under the curtain for it I felt the dog's wet nose on my hand.

'You! What are you doing here?' I said, but I felt pleased to see him again. His tail wagged and swished the curtain.

I picked up the coin and pushed it into the slot. The first of the four photographs flashed and the time on the screen counted down until it was ready for the next. The dog had come into the booth, as if he was wondering what was going on. He stood up on his hind legs as it flashed a second time. I think it scared him a bit because he jumped up on to my lap. I tried to push him out of the way but the camera flashed again and again.

'No, dog, no!' I said as he licked my face. 'You don't need a passport!'

The pictures developed and dropped out of the slot. The first one was okay, but the second had the top of the dog's head at the bottom corner. They would have to do, though. The other two photos were a jumble of my hair and the dog's hair, and me making funny faces because of the dog's wet tongue. They were nice; I liked them and they made me smile. I'd keep those two for myself.

'Lost-property office next,' I said. 'You coming, dog?'

The office was closed when we got there so the dog and I watched the fishing boats coming in instead, inspecting the smells and sights of the baskets and trays that the fishermen unloaded. Spider crabs and lobsters reached out to pinch at the dog's nose and long fur; scales of fish flashed with light in the sun. I asked the dog which fish he might like for his dinner because that was what Grandfather used to ask me.

Eventually the lost-property office opened and I went in.

'I found a passport,' I said, sliding it across the counter. 'It's from a girl called Beth Saunders, aged twelve.'

'That belongs to me!' a voice called out from behind me.

Beth Saunders was about my height, with short brown hair, and she threw herself at the desk, clasping the passport in both hands. 'I didn't want to tell my parents I'd lost it. I've been coming in every five minutes hoping somebody would hand it in.'

I knew how the girl felt. It was just how I was when I went to the post office again and again. The lost-property man rolled his eyes at her, muttering that now, at last, she might stop bothering him.

Beth asked my name and thanked me for finding her passport but as I went to leave she said, 'There's a dog outside, does it belong to you, Azi?'

'No,' I said. I wasn't really interested in talking to tourists who took snapshots of their holiday and collected short-lived souvenirs.

But as I walked away the dog came to my side, following me as usual. Beth ran and caught up with me.

'Are you sure he's not yours, because he looks as if he belongs to you.'

I smiled at that and bent down to ruffle the dog's hair. 'He's been following me around for a few days,' I said. 'But he isn't actually mine.'

'Then he's lost and needs to go home,' Beth said.

I looked at the dog. There were lots of strays on

the island and I hadn't really thought about the dog like that. Beth's words reminded me of Grandfather and how much I missed him and our home. It hurt me inside and I wasn't expecting it. I needed to feel close to the place I belonged.

'I have to go,' I said, running off towards Grandfather's cottage.

Since yesterday I'd been wondering about a lot of new things. For the last two years the only question I'd had was *when* was Grandfather coming back. Now Uncle had said he wasn't, I wanted to see what was going on at the cottage.

Grandfather's cottage was at the end of a narrow road over the other side of the village from Uncle's restaurant. It was where I had grown up. I knew that I hadn't been born in the cottage but that Grandfather had raised me there because my parents had died.

The bench was still outside the cottage by the window where Grandfather used to sit in his cap with his walking stick, indigo tattoo on his bare hairy arm: an anchor coiled with the tentacles of a sea monster. When I was little I used to brush at the hairs of his arm, smoothing them down to see the picture clearly; he'd say, 'It's the two sides of being a man of the sea, Azi. The anchor for feeling steady while the battle with the monster rages.'

Two cottages had been pulled down next to Grandfather's, not long ago, and two were deserted, decaying on the other side. His cottage had walls thick with white paint, which I had always helped him redo every other year. His blue front door was the same bright colour as the scales of paint left on the one I'd found on the sea. After I'd found the passport, I'd started to think about that door.

56

The second sign must be to do with the cottage. Maybe this was where I'd find my birth certificate. That was the last thing that I needed to get a passport, find Grandfather and make him come home.

A small patch of concrete with crazy-shaped cemented stones, painted white round the edges, lay under the sandy dust at the front of the cottage. A pot with dried weeds was by the door and a key still underneath. I hadn't been in there since Grandfather had left because Uncle had said I wasn't allowed to, but now I let myself in and the dog came too.

I remembered the days when I'd find Grandfather asleep in his chair in the gloom at the back of the room, head rolled forward over his chest, several days' growth of silver stubble speckling his slack mouth, his shawl slipped to the floor and an empty glass held loosely in his hands. I looked around at the thinness of the life we'd left behind in the cottage. The walls grim with a crust of paint, the swirls of dust on the tiled floor, the gas bottle and rubber tube to the cooker, the space underneath the wooden staircase where I used to sleep. A bright corner of light poured down the stairs from the window in the bedroom and had been my morning alarm clock.

I rummaged through the cupboard and the chest of drawers, between empty bottles, under Grandfather's bed, under the mattress, behind the wardrobe. Even though I felt sure that I would find it, there was no birth certificate, nothing to say that this was where I came from. Either Grandfather had taken it with him or Uncle must have it somewhere that I hadn't found yet. Or was I still reading the signs all wrong?

The dog sniffed around and then, as I stood there, everything that I had been thinking about, and everything I missed about how things used to be, flooded into my chest like a high tide of home-sickness.

I sat on the rug in front of the chair where Grandfather always sat and sobbed. For a moment I thought I could smell the tang of salt and fish and comfort. I leaned forward and closed my eyes. I thought I might feel his knee to rest against but my head touched an empty place.

'You *must* feel your roots are here, Azi, you *must* feel how you belong to the place where your feet first walked. Don't let anyone else tell you that you don't belong *here* . . .' I remembered Grandfather saying, tapping with his stick on the tiled floor by the kitchen sink. 'It was here you pulled yourself up and took your first unsteady steps in *my* home.'

It was Grandfather I had held on to when I was unsteady; Grandfather whose eyes I had looked into when saltwater had overflowed from his. I longed to be with him, just as I had all the other days. I longed for him here. I belonged in this house with him.

If he wasn't coming back of his own accord, I needed to find a way to bring him back, to anchor myself to him again, to say sorry because it was my fault he had left in the first place.

The dog came and sat beside me and dropped something from his mouth. A dirty old sock. I wiped my eyes and dangled the sock in the air and wondered for a moment if the dog would help me find Grandfather with his nose.

7

Not long before he left, Grandfather had told me that holidays were originally holy days. Days of the divine. He'd crossed himself, looking up, searching, as if God might need reminding that Grandfather was still here.

School holidays used to mean that Grandfather and I could spend more time in his boat, swimming, catching fish and diving. Sometimes together, sometimes with him standing where the waves rolled over his toes while he held the tin bucket, waiting for me to come out of the water with treasure so we could pour it all back where it came from when the sun dived beyond the horizon at night. Now the holidays belonged to tourists, worshippers of a different kind, to people who didn't belong here but were only visitors. They lay on the sand at the washed edges of the land and swam in the very edge of the vast blue sea, not knowing it the way we did.

Once I made friends with a tourist. I was about seven and so was he, but I can't remember his name. We sat where the waves lapped, building sandcastles in the sinking sand, and then when I swam out, and he tried to follow, his parents snatched him away. I saw him at the beach all week but he wasn't allowed to come over to play with me. At the end of the week he was gone and somehow that was worse than not knowing him at all. So, when the girl who'd lost her passport came over when I was at the cove, I didn't really want to see or talk to her. Tourists came for a moment, a blink in time, dissolving away like sand-castles when the sea washed over them but Grandfather and I built our history here. And any day now the girl would be gone soon enough.

'Hi, Azi,' she said, sitting down by me and the dog. 'I'm glad I found you because I wanted to say sorry.'

'What for?' I said as I wasn't expecting that.

She stroked the dog, not looking up at me as if the sun was too bright for her. 'I think I said something to upset you but I truly don't know what it was,' she said.

'No, it was nothing,' I said, not wanting to talk

about how she had reminded me of how I felt lost and wanted to go back home to the cottage where I belonged. I got up and walked along the edge of the water, hoping she would go but she got up too and walked alongside me, the dog following both of us. Beth's hands were behind her back, her head down, looking at the ground right in front of her, as if she had to see every stone or dip in the sand and exactly where to put her feet so she didn't stumble or make a mistake again.

'What are you doing?' I said.

'Thinking,' she said, still walking with me.

'What about?'

'Well . . .' She seemed to be deciding whether to say something or not. 'My family and I have been away from home for a very long time.'

She surprised me again. She told me that her mum and dad went where the work took them.

They rented places wherever they ended up, travelling and living and working around the world in different coastal towns. Beth had been to schools in several different countries. They had a house in London but hadn't been back for years.

'We're staying here for a few months, and . . .' She hesitated again. 'And it's hard to make new friends when you don't end up staying anywhere for very long.'

I was surprised at everything Beth told me. She said that she thought the place where we were born was a part of us but when she tried to describe what that was like for her she couldn't find any words. She said it was difficult to describe to someone from another place but that you didn't even need to say it to someone who was from the same place. It reminded me of what Grandfather had said about our roots.

'My grandfather was a fisherman,' I said. 'He always used to say I came from the sea because of how much I like swimming and diving.'

'I was born in London but I spent most of the first couple of years of my life at sea,' she said, which made me turn and look at her properly. She smiled. 'I love the sea too. My mum said I first learned to walk on our boat so I have good sea legs.' She said it wasn't surprising that anyone loved the sea because her mother had told her that all babies came from watery worlds in the first place. Even before we were given a name, we floated in the water of life.

'Like fish or turtles or dolphins do?' I said, and it made her laugh. Grandfather had always told me, *Azi, you are a beautiful creature from the sea*, even if he was teasing me because of how much I enjoyed being in it. Maybe Beth wasn't a tourist after all, but I wasn't sure what she was. All I knew was up until that moment she hadn't really mattered to me, except as a possible customer for Uncle, but now I felt differently. She was someone I wanted to get to know.

'Do you want to see a turtle nest?' I asked her. As we walked I told her how turtles rode the warm tides and were carried on currents, clockwise, round the Mediterranean. Almost everything they wanted was there in the sea for them so they could roam around and around for years. And then one day they would know they had to go to land to start life again.

I showed her the fenced-off area at the other end of the cove, hidden in a small inlet between rocks so it wasn't visible unless you were right next to it. I told her how the mother turtle found her way back to the same nesting site, every other year, and buried her eggs. The babies would never meet her but as soon as they were born they would instinctively run for the sea, following the same flow that their mother had, knowing without ever being told where they belonged. Then, when they were grown, they would probably come back here to lay their eggs too.

Beth was amazed.

We kneeled down and she stared through the wire, as if any moment now the sand would erupt and baby turtles would pop out. I felt the dog's whiskers tickle my ear as he came and stood between us, sniffing each of us in turn.

'What's the dog called?' Beth said.

'I don't know. He's probably already got a name, so I didn't want to give him another one,' I said.

'Even if he's not yours we should call him something,' she laughed. 'He's company for us for a while and company needs a name.'

She said *us* as if we had made something together, as if she thought we were the same. There were so many things that were different about us but what was the same was the fact that we were not where we felt we belonged.

I told Beth how I'd first met the dog.

'Rocky or Shadow wouldn't really suit him,' she said, twitching her mouth from side to side. The dog turned away and went and sat looking out to sea again.

'He reminds me of a sandcastle,' I said, as the dog sat there, tall but fragile at the edge of the waves, as if soon the tide would wash over him and he'd disappear. 'Like he's made of sand.'

'That's quite a beautiful thought,' Beth said.

We agreed to call him Sandy, not only because of the colour of his coat.

'It'll just be a name we use,' Beth said.

As I watched the dog sitting there I realised he was also a lot like me. And Beth maybe.

All three of us sat together quietly, doing nothing but looking out to sea, and I thought it was possible that we might all be looking for someone we couldn't see.

'I might not be here for the whole holidays,' I told Beth. 'I'm going to London soon.'

I think I might have said something to upset her this time but I didn't know what it was. Beth said she had to go but was wondering on another day, before I went to London, where I might be if she wanted to find me.

'Here,' I said. 'I'm nearly always here.'

8

I SLID THE PASSPORT FORM, SOME MONEY AND THE photos under the counter partition and Mrs Halimeda looked at it all with screwed-up eyes. The form was a bit curly and bent in places from being tucked inside my clothes, and smudged with some pencil marks and rubbings. I told her Uncle had filled it out in a hurry in the kitchen when he was very busy, which seemed a plausible reason for it to look tatty.

'I see,' she said slowly.

'Uncle lost my birth certificate,' I said. 'But he's put a note on the top about that.' I'd written an explanation in capital letters, so it looked as if Uncle had really meant it when he wrote that he'd dropped my birth certificate in the fish soup and it had fallen to bits.

'Yes, I see that too.' She leaned across to Mr Halimeda who was sorting out parcels behind her and whispered, showing him the form. He looked over his glasses at me and then at her.

'How long before it's ready?' I said.

Mr Halimeda was about to say something when Mrs Halimeda held up her hand to stop him. 'A few days,' she answered, a slight sliver of a smile twitching in the corner of her mouth. 'Leave it with me.'

'Oh, I nearly forgot,' I said before I left, 'Uncle

said you must come to the restaurant some time and try his home-made moussaka.' I hoped it would convince her that Uncle knew all about the passport. I knew she wouldn't come and hoped I'd only have to visit once more to pick up the passport when it arrived.

'I'm not going to be around for the whole holidays,' I told Sandy who had been waiting outside the post office.

Sandy's ears twitched and I crouched down beside him. 'Maybe you ought to go home too.' But he didn't go.

When Sandy and I got to the cove, Beth was already there in her swimming costume and sunglasses, sitting cross-legged on a towel with a palm tree printed on it.

'I wasn't sure if you'd gone to London yet,' she said kind of casually, although she laughed a bit nervously. She said she'd only come to the cove because it was her favourite spot so far and she liked that it was quiet and away from everyone else. 'I wasn't following you around or anything but, as you're still here, do you want to go swimming?'

I felt relieved that everything had gone well with the passport. I had nothing to do for a few days while I waited for it to come and Beth might be able to help me work out how to get to London.

'Come on,' I said to Beth and Sandy, stripping off my T-shirt and kicking off my flip-flops. 'We could try to remember the watery worlds where we began.'

Beth was a good swimmer, just as she'd said she was. She seemed so much happier and relaxed in the sea. I told her to be careful where she put her feet because of the sea-urchins that had sharp spines to protect themselves. I dived to the bottom of the water and, in the cool silence, looked up at the shadowed shape of Beth floating on the water, kicking her legs a little, and the bright ripple above her where the sun was. Then we floated together on our backs, Sandy circling us, making hardly a splash with his graceful paddle. The sun was on our bodies as we were held up by the sea, bobbing and rocking like babies in the arms of the waves.

'I think I can remember in a strange kind of way that the place we all came from when we were growing into babies was a perfect place,' Beth said. 'Kind of like our first home.'

'I can't remember anything about that,' I said. 'But I guess it was very nice if it was like this.'

We tried to recall our first memories, but with the sea all around me I could only think of

Grandfather. Beth was remembering and remembering, chatting away about the time she was on their boat and somebody was reading her a story and it was raining – *was it Mum or Dad reading?* And the time she was in the water, bobbing in her life jacket, when a dolphin swam nearby and one of her parents – *it was Dad, definitely Dad!* – held her hand to reach out to try to touch it.

'Maybe our memories know where our real roots are,' I said. 'And maybe it's places like the sea that make us feel good because of how we began.'

'Even when we are like drifting weed?' she said.

I smiled. 'Even drifting like this we are a kind of life raft.'

I collected the door from the beach and let it float in the shallows while Beth climbed on to it with the tin bucket, and I heaved Sandy up with her. I swam, kicking my legs, pushing the door out past the rocky end of the beach, and then I dived to the bottom. I rummaged through the sand, disturbing scallops that clapped like castanets, pulsing through the water to get away, and I swam among small fish as they fast-forwarded into life, darting and wriggling. I collected empty shells, interesting stones and small pieces of seaweed to make a miniature version of the sea in my tin bucket, handing everything up to Beth on the door, Sandy inspecting it all too.

'What's it all for?' Beth said.

'Wait and see,' I said. Maybe she would under-stand. I held on to the door and kicked again, pushing Sandy, Beth and the bucket back to the shore. I filled the bucket with seawater and they watched as I poured in handfuls of sand like a waterfall of golden sugar before it all eventually settled on the bottom. I put in all the other sea treasures and caught a crab about the size of a coin and let it sink into the new world.

Sandy wandered off. He shook the water from his fur and sat near the edge of the sea, just watching. Beth wanted to keep looking at the mini aquarium and so did I. When I peered into the small world, with its small pieces of things from the sea, it made me feel kind of steady.

'I still don't know what it is,' Beth said.

It was hard to describe it to her. I'd never had to explain anything to Grandfather. He'd always seemed to know too. I thought of all the seas and oceans, all the creatures we couldn't see, roaming in and roaming out on the tides. On the map at school, somebody had coloured the seas and oceans in different shades of blue and called them different names.

'You see the sea here?' I pointed out to what lay

in front of us, wide and blue, sparkling, softly washing the shore. 'It's part of a bigger sea called the Mediterranean, which is joined through a narrow seaway between Europe and Africa to an even bigger ocean called the Atlantic. But, really, each ocean and sea is part of the same giant water-world that covers most of the Earth. Joined together but divided up.'

If Beth already knew this, she didn't say. She sat back up, put her elbows on her knees, resting her face in her hands, and listened. 'Go on,' she said.

'Well, this world in the bucket is like a very small sea,' I said, peering in. 'It's got everything the big sea has but it's all by itself.' I carried it down to the shoreline, Beth following, and poured it all gently back into the sea, the tiny little crab swirling with the water. 'Now, it's with everything, all of the sea, where it really belongs.'

We sat down with Sandy and gazed out at what we couldn't see beyond the horizon or the surface. Beth didn't say anything more but stroked Sandy now and again.

'I think I get it,' she said. 'Is that why you want to go to London? Because it's where you belong?'

'No, it's because my grandfather is there,' I said. 'I'm not sure how to get to him, though.'

Beth told me I'd have to take a ferry to the mainland to get to the airport, and then catch a flight to London. London was a huge place, she said, but as long as I had his address I should be able to find him. I didn't tell her that I didn't have his address – that I had no idea where he was living.

A ferry was making its way across the sea and it wouldn't be long before it was time for me to go down to the quay to hand out leaflets. Beth carried on talking.

'Sometimes I feel like I'm a tourist, even when I'm at home in London, except there isn't as much sunshine as here and the main river is brown,' she said. 'There are millions and millions of people in London but I'm happy here because . . .' She looked at me and then at Sandy and then away, stretching out her legs so her toes were in the water. 'Because here we've got the sea all around us and it's the same sea touching all the other places in the world.'

It was hard to describe that feeling, but she had done a good job.

9

I THOUGHT A LOT ABOUT WHAT BETH HAD SAID.
I was also surrounded by many people a lot of
the time – in the restaurant, down on the quay
– but the rest of the time I was at the cove on
my own. I wanted to feel like I belonged to the
crowds, to the people who lived here, but I also
felt like I couldn't, not without Grandfather
here too. He knew me in a way that nobody

else did and, without him, I was lost. Beth seemed to end up saying something that reminded me how much I hurt inside, how much I missed being with Grandfather, although she hadn't meant to.

I pushed the stakes in firmer round the turtle nest, piled sand and pressed with my heel, remembering the day when the sourness had really got into Grandfather. His hand had trembled round his glass of grog, his eyelids blinking slow and heavy.

'I caught you like a fish, Azi,' he had said, his eyes glazed with mystery and fear, as if monsters were rousing from deep caves at the bottom of his sea of mirages. The bottles of grog he drank made his memories and dreams merge into one, like the shadows of the night. In the dark, the hump of a wave could look like the dive of a dolphin, and the moon on calm water could look like a solid path. I'd moved the bottle out of Grandfather's reach when he'd muttered and cried.

'Why do they still say I don't belong here?' I'd asked him yet again. 'Where am I from? Where do I belong?'

'You came from the sea, Azi,' he'd said again, and for the first time I'd felt angry, his sodden talk making me feel as if I was standing on quick-sand.

He'd reached for the bottle but I had got up and moved to the other side of the room, taking the grog with me. Grandfather had risen like a wave, rolling tall and fearsome, reaching not for me but as if he could drown the space between us. Our hands gripped the bottle.

'That's the grog talking, Grandfather,' I said. 'The grog can't tell me where I came from!'

But Grandfather's eyes were lost in a sea mist, his ears to the roar of the waves. Uncle had said somebody needed to stop his grog-consuming and they'd fallen out, barely speaking to each other, and I had kept quiet when Uncle had thought Grandfather had stopped.

'Shall I ask Uncle instead?' I'd said to Grandfather. 'Shall I tell him you can't tell me where I'm really from because you're drinking too much?'

I shouldn't have said it. Shocking us both, we let go of the bottle. It dropped and smashed, fragments of glass and gold liquid spraying out for a sharp moment while Grandfather stumbled, falling back.

'Grandfather!' I kneeled, felt a shard of glass stick into my knee and got back up, shuffling round behind him to put my arms under his armpits to heave him upright.

'Leave me, leave me,' he said, offering no strength to try to move.

I sat down behind him and let his head and shoulders lean against me. The grog seeped into his trousers and the rag rug, and spread itself to a thin shiny puddle across the floor.

Grandfather slept, drooping and sobering with my arms round his chest, my fingers linked to stop him from sliding sideways.

'Why do people say I don't belong here, Grandfather?' I whispered.

I felt like the shell of a turtle, protecting the soft inside of Grandfather where the truth about where I came from, and where my roots were, lay pickled in spirits. Grandfather said I came from the sea but he said my roots were in the cottage with him where we lay on the tiled floor against the kitchen cupboards.

For hours we had lain there like that, before Grandfather patted my hands. All the anger had gone and he weighed heavy with sorrow and pity, maybe for not knowing why he was on the floor.

'What time is it, Azi?'

I didn't have a watch but I looked over at the staircase where the sun was squinting into the cottage through the bedroom window. A thin white sunspot lay across the top step.

'Five o'clock,' I said, as minutes or an hour here and there didn't seem to matter. 'Do you want to get up yet? Remember we were going to the cove so I could show you what I found.' I'd wanted him to see the turtle.

Grandfather patted my leg and, pulling his hand away, looked at the blood on his fingers.

'What have I done?' he cried.

'It's nothing,' I said, because the cut on my knee didn't hurt anywhere near as much as the pain I felt in hurting him.

'Hold still a minute,' he said. Gently he picked out the splinter of glass and shed tears while he bathed my blood away and cried again over monsters from the deep that I could not see. He held my feet in his hands, rubbed them as if he could feel again the roots that connected me to him.

'I have become a monster silver fish, Azi,' he said.

'No!' I said. 'You're a man of the sea and one day you will be strong enough to reel the monster in.'

I saw the change in him right then, as if he was leaving the story of us because he couldn't finish it, because I had taken his strength from him.

'I think I need to be by myself for a while now,' he said.

Uncle had said family needed him in London. But I knew it was my fault Grandfather left the next day.

10

I HAD MANY OTHER MEMORIES BESIDES THOSE ONES – of Grandfather raising me well, of knowing nothing but us and our world and what the sea taught us. But he was lost now, all at sea, far, far across the sea. That day, I'd hurt the only person that meant everything to me. I had to tell him I was sorry. I knew that now.

When Beth went back to her family that evening

Sandy stuck with me, like he was on a long piece of elastic, bouncing back if I went too far away. But when we got to the restaurant he hovered within the shadows, as if he knew that he wouldn't be popular if he was seen.

The night whirred with insects. The restaurant was empty and dark but for a few bulbs strung up in the grapevines overhead. Uncle was sitting at a table on the deck with Maria.

'Hey, Azi. Come and sit here,' Maria said sweetly. 'Remember what I said,' she told Uncle firmly. She got up and said goodnight to both of us but went inside instead of going home, tidying up things that were already tidy, wiping surfaces that were already clean.

I knew I was in trouble when I saw Uncle's arm was lying across the table with my passport application underneath it.

Uncle brushed the crumbs from the table into his palm and straightened the tablecloth. 'Mrs Halimeda paid me a visit.'

I was expecting yelling but instead he got up and straightened all the chairs round the next table, as if the precise position of them was very important. 'Did I teach you to do these kinds of things?' he said, picking up the form and waving it. 'To deceive people?'

Maria coughed from inside the restaurant as he lay the form on the table and sat back down. I pulled it towards me, seeing clearly now how Mrs Halimeda hadn't been fooled.

'This is the kind of thing Grandfather taught you, isn't it?' Uncle said. 'To go behind my back.'

'No!' I said, feeling the need to defend him yet again, saying it louder than I meant to. 'You kept saying he would be coming back but he still hasn't come.'

'Because he's not coming back!' Uncle said, his words exploding and hanging in the air, like a cloud laden with a storm, like the breath I held, because it was Uncle who was the one who had deceived me for two years. He closed his eyes and rubbed at his head.

Everything I had tried to do to go to London, all the hoping and the signs in the sea that I thought I had seen, had come to nothing. It was only now, with Uncle holding back from yelling, that he left enough room for me to say what I needed to say.

'I want to see him. I need to see him . . .' My voice trailed away. 'I want to go to London.'

Uncle looked towards Maria again, and she nodded, encouraging him to say something.

Wearily he rubbed his face before finally saying, 'He's not in London.'

Stung again, I pinched my lips together, staring and glaring at him to see if he was deceiving me again.

'I don't know where he is, Azi. He didn't tell me where he was going. I said he was in London because it was the first thing that came into my head.'

'So he could be anywhere!' I yelled. I couldn't hold back what burned like acid inside my heart. I grabbed the passport form and photos and, not wanting anyone to see what was spilling out of me, ran down the beach and over the rocks to the cove, running faster when Maria called my name and Uncle yelled, 'He hasn't contacted me. He hasn't told me where he is! It's the truth this time, Azi!'

Swimming at night was the only thing that helped me sleep. When the sea was glossy black with a zebra-striped path of the moon flickering across it, while everything was black and white in the light of the moon, shades of dark grey and gloom, I could try to forget. Sandy wouldn't come swimming with me at first (did he feel there were monsters he couldn't see in the dark?) but stood on the shoreline, looking down at the waves, as if he thought it was hopeless being only on the edge of the sea too. I dived into the depths with the quietness of the deep. I burst up through the surface when my lungs fought to move with the rhythm of life again. With my body in the sea and my head in the air, my chest relaxed into the same flow of the sea breathing against the land, against me. Then I lay, rocking in the arms of the waves. Unsteady. Drifting.

But more at home than any other place without Grandfather.

Was I never going to see him again? How was I going to feel I belonged to any place on the land without him here? I must have hurt him so much for him to go and not want to come back. I had to tell him I was sorry but how was I ever going to be able to do that?

I got cold and sat by the turtle's nest with a towel wrapped round me. Grandfather wasn't where Uncle had told me he had been all this time. He had been telling me for two years that he was in London and that he'd be back, just not yet. But that was only a small part of a bigger story that Grandfather wasn't here to tell or to finish.

Litter had floated in on the tide and lay scattered along parts of the cove. I wandered the sands, picking up the rubbish. The sea had already cleaned my footprints from the beach, and the dog and I made new trails on the edge of the waves, where our different footprints softly disappeared in the wet sand.

'Uncle taught me to clean up the beach for the sake of the restaurant, Sandy,' I said to the dog as he stood by me. But it was Grandfather who taught me to keep the beach clean for the creatures of the sea, like the turtle. And it was Grandfather that taught me to look to the sea for signs; how I was raised would always be with me, even if I tried to think like Uncle.

I sifted through the rubbish, looking for anything that connected me to Grandfather. I found a wine bottle, still with a cork in it, and poured out the contents. I rolled up the tatty passport application and the two photos and stuffed them inside the bottle and put the cork back in. I climbed up on the rocks to the highest part that jutted out into the sea and I spun round, faster and faster until I felt all my strength was in the hand that held the bottle. I let it all go. The bottle flew through the air and landed on the pull of the tide. It bobbed and swayed, drifting slowly away. *A message from me to you, Grandfather. Please come home where you belong.*

I went to bed, my ear to the sound of the sea washing in through the window. And with it came another sound. Sandy whistled a soft, sad song into the breeze.

11

I HARDLY SLEPT THAT NIGHT, AND GOT UP EARLY and swam, trying to wash away dreams of searching for Grandfather. But how could I when he was all my waking-up too? I went to Grandfather's cottage again, to be where I felt I was closest to him.

Trying to be the way Uncle wanted me to be was hard. I didn't mind doing the jobs he gave me, living at the restaurant, and the life that came and went with it. But it had never felt like home. Uncle had been raised in Grandfather's cottage before me. Uncle had pulled himself up at the kitchen cupboards when he had learned to walk as a baby, and ended up by a kitchen cooker. Was that where I would end up too?

It was like trying to be someone that I wasn't. It was like changing all I could be. I really didn't belong anywhere on the land, just like the children at school had told me. I didn't feel like I was from the place where I was living. I just wanted to go home, to the cottage, to be with Grandfather, where I did belong. We spoke the same language of the sea, a kaleidoscope of amazing stories woven through us.

Back at the cottage, I felt only what was missing. I looked again at what had been left behind. The spilled grog hadn't been cleaned up properly and my flip-flops still crackled on a sticky patch on the floor. Some of the broken glass still glinted in the corners, the sheets on Grandfather's bed were tangled as if he had struggled while he was sleeping and left in a hurry to escape a nightmare. The fridge smelled. I cleaned up. I did what Uncle had taught me, what I naturally did when I was with Grandfather. I washed dishes, scrubbed the floor, swept the stones outside the door and straightened Grandfather's bed. The cottage had no pictures or keepsakes. Nothing Grandfather had held on to was visible. For a moment it felt lifeless, but as I stood there, looking at everything that was familiar, I remembered us and our lives: eating fish freshly caught, cooked on a griddle pan, taking a teaspoon of honey after and savouring it – *Honey is good for you inside and out.* I'd lie under the water in the bath, looking up at him through the ripples. The golden sun in my blue sky.

I hadn't meant to hurt Grandfather. I would never have told Uncle that Grandfather was drinking the grog again, ever since he lost his fishing boat. I might have threatened it but I'd never have done it and more than anything I wished I'd never said it. That's what had made him leave. I'd seen how Grandfather had been eased for a while by a scrap of laughter and joy when he raised his glass and his spirits had risen. We could live like that again. An old fisherman and a creature from the sea.

I hoped the message in the bottle would reach Grandfather. My message would be a sign to him that I was looking for him, that I was sorry, that I wanted him to come back. I didn't know how else to make him come home.

The quay was busy that afternoon. Water gurgled against the harbour wall and between the ferries and fishing boats tethered with swaying ropes. A huge cruise ship had moored offshore with a thousand small dark portholes in white high-rise hulls. A floating city. Smaller boats brought passengers from the ship and Sandy and I joined the crowds, Sandy sniffing people, me handing out leaflets as they stepped ashore and offshore.

On autopilot I called out, 'Genuine Greek dishes. Home-made kebabs. Ice-cold drinks on the beach.'

Sandy and I hung around in the timetable kiosk. We watched ferries arrive and leave, breathing oily, salty air, reading timetables for something to do, my eyes constantly scanning outside, just in case, for an old man from the sea.

Then Beth turned up.

'Did you know that there's a place in the ocean called the Mariana Trench?' she said as if we'd been together, talking the whole time. 'It's somewhere near Japan, and it's deeper than the height of Everest, which is the highest place on Earth.'

'No, I didn't know that,' I said, but I liked that she had brought with her a small piece of information about the sea.

'I've got something for Sandy,' she said.

She didn't ask where we'd been and, although I had been trying to avoid her, I suddenly felt glad she was there, chatting away about how nice it was to have bumped into us. She'd brought Sandy some chicken and we sat on a bench, Sandy in front of us. Beth thought the dog might need some kind of training but he sat at our feet, tail swishing, ears pricked, nose twitching and glistening, soft eyes on Beth's hand, not snatching at the food, waiting patiently for his reward. I began to think that he had come from a good home where somebody had taught him to behave himself. He ate all of the chicken and then turned round, nose in the air, staring out to sea again. Another ferry arrived and Sandy went over to sniff at everyone.

'I think he misses someone,' Beth said. 'It's kind of obvious now I think about it.'

I had a lot in common with that dog.

I decided we ought to take Sandy to the lost-property office, although people didn't hand in things that were alive, whining and homesick. I guessed Sandy lived here on the island and it didn't make sense that somebody didn't want him. He'd probably wandered off and forgotten how to get back.

We had to push Sandy through the door because he was reluctant to go in, wanting to sit outside, probably watching to see if his owner passed by. Beth asked if the office was for lost dogs and the man sighed because it was Beth again.

'No dogs,' the man said.

The man didn't look at Sandy so we picked him up, holding either end so his face was above the counter.

'Has anyone been in and said they've lost *this* dog?' Beth said.

Sandy's ears drooped even further down and he seemed embarrassed about being picked up and shoved halfway on the counter like he was in a Punch and Judy show.

The man looked over his glasses. 'Not to my knowledge,' he said.

Beth turned to me and winked. 'I think we should come in every hour until we find his owner, Azi,' she said, nodding with half a grin, which I returned with a whole grin when I worked out what she was doing.

'Every fifteen minutes, maybe,' I said.

The man sighed at the thought he would be pestered again and again by us and slid a piece of paper across the counter. 'Fill this form out as best you can,' he said.

We wrote down a description of the lost property we had found: sad, sandy-coloured dog with wispy fur, long and quite thin, well trained, with a lot of longing in him to go home. I pinned one of my passport photos to the form, of Sandy and me in the booth when he had jumped up on my lap. We left Beth's mother's mobile phone number with the man and he said he would call if he heard anything, but we weren't to hold our breath.

'Azi can hold his breath for a very long time – I've seen him underwater,' Beth said and the man sighed.

Afterwards we wandered along the quay.

'Did you know that an octopus has three hearts?' I said.

'I wonder what that feels like.' Beth clasped her hands round her chest, and then pretended to explode, laughing at herself. 'I think baby octopuses must feel very happy.'

It made me smile. 'I'd rather be a squid,' I said. 'When they are in danger they can camouflage themselves and make it look as if they belong to anything.'

'People eat squid,' she said, pulling a face. 'I had some with chips and mayonnaise,' which made me laugh a lot.

It felt nice doing something with Beth and Sandy, being able to talk about these things without feeling that I was the odd one out.

12

Beth, Sandy and I went to the cove again and she floated on the door with the dog and the bucket while I dived and collected objects from the sea. I stayed in so long that Beth said I ought to come out of the water because I might dissolve like a sugar cube. It was kind of how I felt when I was swimming and I told her that.

'Then I would be mixed in with the huge watery world, just like we began,' I said.

'And maybe you'd make it taste sweet instead of salty,' she said.

I handed her the starfish I'd found, climbed up on the door and made a new aquarium while we rocked gently on the top of the waves. Inside, the bucket looked like a marine flowerbed and we all gazed into the water-world I'd made. For a little while it was the whole world for the starfish, a small world separated from something much bigger. When I tipped it all back into the sea I felt my breath let out all the way from the bottom of my lungs when I saw how the starfish was back where it belonged.

When Beth went home I sat with Sandy at the cove by the turtle nest, and decided I wouldn't avoid Beth any more. When all three of us were sharing our feelings of longing and homesickness it didn't seem so bad. The trouble was the whole time we were together we were also getting closer and closer to a time we'd be apart because all of us were waiting for the day to come when we were back where we belonged too.

'Please let me cut your hair,' Maria said when I got to the restaurant. 'You've got such a nice face and all we can see is your nose sticking out like a little rock among the seaweed.'

I remembered sitting on Grandfather's chair when he did the same, him on a stool with his comb and scissors, me with a towel round my shoulders and a bowl on my head – to help make the edges neat, he'd said.

'Grandfather told me Samson had long hair, that's what made him strong,' I said.

Maria folded her arms and leaned her head on the side. 'I don't think it was Samson's hair,' she said. 'In the end it was Samson's devotion that made him strong enough to overcome things, in the same way your loyalty to Grandfather also gives you strength.' Maria held my shoulders and made me face her. 'You know I think the world of Uncle, heaven only knows why.' She smiled, then sighed. 'But he hasn't been around children much and forgets he's not just the boss of the kitchen and has other roles to fulfil, including looking out for you. But he tries.'

'I know,' I said.

'And you know all that because Grandfather raised you to be considerate and tolerant and patient.'

I looked up at her and it suddenly occurred to me how much loyalty she had to all of us. She had been in and around our lives ever since I could remember. She had often called at Grandfather's cottage with a plate of food left over from the kitchen for him. She'd always had a thing for Uncle and had also kept an eye out for me. She had ties to all of us but who was she most loyal to?

'Maria, do you know where Grandfather is?' I asked her.

She stood up straight and bit the corner of her lip. I could tell instantly by her reaction that she knew something.

'Please tell me,' I said. 'I need to see him. I really do. I don't think he will come home unless I tell him I want him to.' She frowned but I didn't want to explain any more than that. 'He belongs here on the island, Maria. At his cottage. With me.'

'I don't know where he is, but . . .' She hesitated,

chewing on her fingernails. 'But I did see him the morning he left.'

'Where was he going?' I said, hope surging in me.

'I really don't know.' She pushed the hair away from my eyes. 'I saw him down at the quay. He had a ticket for a ferry to one of the islands, but I don't know which one.'

There were twenty-four islands that the ferry went to from here. All I had to do was visit each one and look for him. Grandfather was a man of the sea. He wouldn't be far from the water.

13

THE RESTAURANT WAS BUSIER THAN EVER THE next day, tourists in and out all day, the kitchens sweating, steaming and sizzling, the day roaring with heat. I didn't think I should tell Uncle that I wanted to go searching the islands for Grandfather. He might try to stop me.

Sandy and I walked down the beach and climbed over the rocks. We were sitting at the cove and I was thinking about what to do when Beth came and joined us.

'Have you ever heard of Atlantis?' she said.

I hadn't.

'Dad said it was supposed to be a rich and powerful city built on an island somewhere out there.' She stood, her hand over her eyes, gazing out to the horizon. She chatted away about Atlantis, a place that was supposed to have been perfect. It was interesting, a bit like hearing stories from Grandfather, but his always ended with something amazing and marvellous that he'd seen or learned from the sea. Everything about the place I belonged with Grandfather had been perfect to me. But I had gone and spoiled it all. When that grog bottle smashed into hundreds of pieces it had also shattered everything I'd had with Grandfather along with it. I knew Beth didn't mean to, but she kept reminding me of how bad I felt about what I'd done to Grandfather.

'Atlantis isn't actually a real place, though. It's a story from a long, long time ago that people thought up,' she said. 'Guess what happened to Atlantis?'

'Something awful happened and then it was gone,' I mumbled.

'So you *do* know about it,' she said, surprising me and plonking herself down on the sand beside me to finish the story. 'The people of Atlantis had everything they wanted but then there was a war with another country and they got defeated and then Atlantis sank to the bottom of the sea in an earthquake.' While she talked, she scraped and piled sand up into a small mountain.

'What was the point of the story?' I said, disappointed I had known how it would turn out.

'It's supposed to be a story people can tell each other so that everyone can try to think how to create a perfect place for themselves.' She hesitated, kicking out her foot and flattening the pile of sand before saying, 'Only it seems nobody has succeeded yet.'

I felt the pull of the sea washing me clean of the thoughts of what had gone wrong.

'Do you want to see a wreck?' I said, changing the subject.

Beth's eyes lit up. 'That sounds interesting. Yes, I do.'

I swam, pushing the door with Sandy and Beth on top, along the cove a bit further. The water was fairly shallow so I could stand on the rocks, guiding the raft to the next cove. Shadows made wavy patterns like white fire in the sand beneath the shimmer of the sunlight on the waves. We held our breath and dived down. That first rush through the surface of the sea, the bubbling in my ears and the clean, cool wash over my skin made me feel more at home. Clear and light, the water was see-through, a liquid lens to another world. Sandy paddled around above us, a dog-shaped shadow rippling with the light.

Below us, half buried under shifting sands, was a small fishing boat. It lay on its side, the curve of its ribs cracked, disintegrating, some edges sanded smooth by the rolling tide. Round the prow a flaking painted picture on the hull was still visible: an anchor coiled with the tentacles of a sea monster, the same as Grandfather's tattoo. It was once his fishing boat, and when we'd been in it I had felt like I belonged with him too. It wasn't exactly a place and moved with the sea, but it was where our story and our history grew together, where time linked me to him.

Now the boat was a marine bed for growing coral

shaped like fans, flowers and pipes, netting and feathers, for weeds, small fish and big fish, coloured and striped, and for shelled and spiny creatures. Grandfather's boat had become part of the seabed, recreated for a new underwater life where it had gone down.

Beth and I surfaced and climbed out. I explained to Beth how it had been Grandfather's boat, and how sad he had been when it had sunk.

'What happened?' she asked.

I couldn't tell her about the sea monster that Grandfather told me had sunk it. I didn't think she'd believe me.

'He crashed into the rocks by mistake,' I said.

I also didn't tell her that Grandfather had taken up the grog soon after that, drinking himself into misery. He had been homesick for the sea without his boat.

'How did he catch fish without a boat?' she asked.

'That was the problem; he couldn't any more.'

Sandy had been looking longingly out to sea and now came over, sat down in front of us and sighed. For the first time he looked me in the eyes and I thought I knew something else about him . . .

He already had a perfect place.

At that moment a pelican came flying in from the sea and landed on the beach. As soon as Sandy saw it his ears pricked and his tail began to wag slowly as if he wanted to play. The pelican took off again, but hovered just above us, its beak reminding me of the hammock where Grandfather and I had afternoon naps in the summer. And then Sandy suddenly leaped up, easing out of all his stiffness to jump high, barking a dog's song of joy.

I jumped up. 'Sandy's already got an Atlantis!'

'Tell me! Tell me!' Beth said, dancing around

the sand with me, wanting a bigger story as we all leaped to the sky.

'Sandy doesn't need a *new* perfect home! All he wants is to go to the home that he came from.'

'I thought we already knew that,' Beth said, standing now with her hands on her hips.

'No, don't you see?' I couldn't say exactly what I meant, not yet. 'We need to find Sandy's home,' I said.

'I thought we were already doing that too,' Beth said, a puzzled look crossing her face as she reminded me about the lost-property office.

I had to tell her the bigger plan, having to explain first that I wasn't going to London any more, that Grandfather wasn't there after all, that Uncle didn't know where he was but that I was trying to find him.

'Sandy might have come from one of the islands!

And even if he didn't, I could tell Uncle that Sandy had come over on a ferry and been accidentally left behind,' I said. 'Uncle doesn't want me to find Grandfather but I don't have to tell him I'm looking. All I need to do is buy a ticket and take Sandy with me. That way I could tell Uncle I would be looking for Sandy's owner, when all the time I would actually be looking for Grandfather.'

Beth looked even more confused. 'But why doesn't your uncle want you to find him?' she asked slowly.

I ignored her as my plan became complete in my head. Sandy would help me find Grandfather. I was sure of it!

14

Beth said my plan had some problems. They
included me not telling the whole truth to Uncle.
Wasn't that the same as telling lies? I didn't tell
her that Uncle had been telling lies himself by
saying that Grandfather was in London when he
wasn't and telling me that he was coming back
soon. I was determined I knew exactly what to
do now.

I did wonder why my plan was bothering Beth so much. She scratched her head and walked up and down, turning and trying to place her feet carefully in the footprints she had already made. She said she wasn't sure I should be deceitful but I wasn't sure why that mattered to her. I would be the one who was in trouble if Uncle found out. Not Beth. And then I worked out what it was that was really bothering her.

'Why don't you come with us?' I said.

'Well, I thought . . .' she said.

'I mean I want you to come, but I wasn't sure you wanted to,' I said, and it all felt a bit awkward for a minute.

'It's not being *us* to tell lies,' she said, then ducked her head down and for the fourth time retraced her footprints, leaving me to wonder again about what she was actually trying to say.

I told her she wouldn't be telling lies because the true purpose of *her* journey would be to find Sandy's home. What if he had come from one of the islands? It seemed to make a lot of sense that he had. And for me, Grandfather was my Atlantis. Would a small deception really matter when Grandfather was my perfect place? I had to find him. She seemed to understand that, saying one day she'd go home and be with all the friends she grew up with and she was sure that it would feel the same.

By that evening Beth was completely in on the plan and I was convinced by then that the reason Sandy had come to the quay and been staring out to sea was because he knew his home was *across* the sea. Beth had decided that as Sandy was also looking for his Atlantis it was a good enough truth not to feel bad that either of us was deceiving anyone. She completely included herself in what I was doing. It was *us* all the way.

Beth brought her parents to eat at Uncle's restaurant that night. She had already told them about Sandy who was hovering in the shadows nearby. He must have been very well trained by his owner as he just lay there, only his tufty eyebrows twitching as he watched us. Beth's parents had agreed that she could go on ferry trips with me, but, because of the sort of person Beth was, she also wanted to speak to Uncle herself. It seemed to me as though she had to make sure that Uncle was all right with her and what she was doing. By the end of the evening, when most people had left, and Beth's family were drinking coffee and the kitchens had simmered down, I took her out the back to meet him.

'Call me Uncle,' he said when she stuttered over what name to use, and she beamed at being instantly welcomed into the family. 'You enjoyed the squid?'

'The best,' she said, rubbing her stomach. 'Crispy and chewy and delicious.'

Uncle winked and offered her a dish of nutty baklava dripping with honey, and I had to stop myself mentioning Grandfather who gave me a spoonful of honey every day, rubbed it on sore skin and swore by it to remedy ailments inside and out. Beth licked hard at her sticky lips, making all the kinds of noises that Uncle liked to hear. She asked Uncle to come out and meet her parents and they talked together about what we had asked. Her parents said that we could visit three islands but then after that we had to leave Sandy's fate to others. Uncle agreed with them.

Only three *islands.*

Beth bit her lip.

'That'll be fine,' Beth said, nudging me and the disappointment out of my face. 'We'll be helping the man at the lost-property office too by not going in there,' Beth said. 'He'd be very fed up if we went in all the time and kept asking about the dog.'

Uncle stared hard at me and, disappointed as I was, I had to steer him clear of thinking too hard about it all.

'We'd be helping you and your restaurant too, Uncle,' I said. 'We don't want stray dogs around here, do we?'

'We've got a timetable so we could tell you exactly which ferry we're on,' Beth said. We told them we'd go to the lost-property offices on the island quays and leave the dog's details there and hopefully find his owners. I let Beth do a lot of the talking because she was good at that, and I thought it would sound better coming from Beth rather than from me.

Although Beth's parents were happy that Beth was sensible, that she'd grown up being independent and worldly-wise, Uncle hesitated about even three trips.

Maria came over and asked what we were up to. I looked to her to see what she might say, guessing she might have some idea of what else I had in mind. 'Why don't I see them off in the morning?' she said. 'I can call by the quay before coming to work and make sure they get on the ferry safely.' She knew the timetables for the morning ferries that left and the afternoon ferries that arrived. She knew people we could call on at other islands to look out for us if necessary. She didn't give anything away about Grandfather but maybe because she hadn't worked that out herself. Uncle was still stalling, though. Who was going to go down to the quay and tell customers about the restaurant?

'I'll take a whole bag of flyers with me,' I said. 'I can give them to everyone on the ferry. You'll have hundreds and hundreds of people coming here, Uncle.'

Beth said it was a brilliant idea and I saw Uncle softening, nodding, Beth's parents agreeing, and Maria nudging Uncle to say yes too.

'Okay,' he said finally. 'But don't be late for work tomorrow, Maria,' he said before going back to the kitchen to make us some lunch to take with us.

While Beth's parents finished their drinks Beth and I checked on Sandy. He was fast asleep but stirred when we sat down, lifting his head to lie across our laps. I hadn't really thought about where he'd been sleeping at night, although I whispered to Beth that he probably went to the cove and sheltered under the door. The nights were so warm that I was sure he would be happier out in the open where it was cooler with the breeze skimming off the waves. He'd looked out to sea every moment he was awake, and he probably felt happier that was the first thing he saw when he opened his eyes in the morning.

As we sat there Sandy whimpered in his dreams, his long, thin legs twitching and paddling, and I wondered if he was dreaming of swimming or of running to someone. Beth lay her hands gently on him because she thought something comforting would pierce through his dreaming and let him know he was all right where he was, for now, and that somebody safe was waiting for him when he woke up to take him home.

'More than anything, I can't bear for him to feel he's alone in his dog dream,' she said.

I knew Beth didn't mean to hurt me when she said things like that, but I couldn't help feeling the longing and homesickness deep inside me all over again, the sharp pain I felt when people told me I didn't belong here. I thought of all the nights I dreamed of Grandfather, of him sinking beneath the waves before I could reach him. I'd wake up, breathless, having dived deep in the dream dark to find him. But as I looked across at Beth and Sandy I felt a small growing sense of belonging to them too.

'He's not alone,' I whispered, 'he's got us for now.'

15

'WHICH ISLAND FIRST?' BETH SAID THE NEXT morning, grinning and holding Sandy's muzzle in her hands and kissing his head.

We'd been waiting at the quay an hour before we needed to be there. We had a huge backpack of lunch that Uncle had made (including scraps for Sandy). I'd brought the tin bucket with me too. Beth didn't ask why I'd brought it but she smiled, as if she understood in her own way. She opened up the folded timetable and showed it to Sandy, thinking he'd make a decision by touching it with his nose.

Maria arrived. Her cousin worked at the ticket kiosk and she had a quick chat with her about making sure we got back safely, whispering to me afterwards that her cousin hadn't been working there two years ago so she hadn't any information for me about Grandfather. I thanked Maria quietly and promised her it wouldn't be long before she could cut my hair. Maria also talked to some of the crew from the ferries who were washing decks and waiting on the quayside for their passengers. She asked them to keep an eye on us too. I wasn't too worried about anyone finding out who I was really searching for because we had the undercover dog story.

Beth was still trying to get Sandy to choose from the timetable, but he kept turning his head away from the paper in front of his face. I'd been thinking of which island Grandfather was most likely to be living on. We had three chances out of twenty-four islands. I hadn't stopped thinking about where he might be, that somehow I would know.

'Have you decided where you're going?' Maria said.

I was almost bursting with the feeling that I was right. 'Two tickets for Chelona!' I said to Maria's cousin.

Maria double-checked the timetable. 'The ferry comes back from Chelona at half past four; make sure you're on it so Uncle has nothing to yell about. Stay around the quay and see if you can find Andreas. He's a fisherman.' She winked. 'He knows all the comings and goings on the island.' I smiled back at her. She was trying to help me find Grandfather, but I understood how she might be uncomfortable about not being loyal to Uncle.

'Why Chelona?' Beth said as we boarded and weaved quickly in and out of other passengers so we could sit on the bench at the front of the top deck.

'Fishermen call it Turtle Island because there's a turtle nesting site there,' I said. 'I have a good feeling it's the kind of place that Grandfather would really like.' I had a feeling too that he'd want to be near creatures of the sea because he loved them.

The journey took nearly an hour, but time whizzed past as Beth and I got to know each other more and more. My hair streamed out behind me, making Beth laugh. She rested her cheek on her arms on the railings, smiling and blinking harder as the ferry speeded up. She told me I looked like a merboy with seaweed hair. You feel exactly like what people call you.

We talked and talked about how a place like Atlantis might look if we built it today. Like the ancient Greek cities, it would have stone walls, strong pillars, golden-white in the sun, friezes carved into patterns and the stories of our lives and history. Our place would bubble with life, friendship and community on glossy marble pavements that would make us feel as if we were walking on water. Towers, arches, walls, climbing straight and tall, and fountains, parks with pools and heaven-seeking palm trees. An island for us surrounded by the sea so we could tumble down the beach in ten running steps to the water that we loved. We got lost in our plan engineered from our own ideas of a perfect place.

'It would be grown from the seeds of people of might and beauty, like us,' Beth said.

It was exciting thinking and talking about it, about us in a place that we had created, with all the feelings of it belonging to us. But the whole time I felt what was missing from it all.

'I wouldn't even mind living under a door on the beach if only Grandfather was there with me,' I said, putting my arm round Sandy.

'You'll find him, Azi,' Beth said. 'You said you lived with him. Where?'

'I'll show you his cottage sometime,' I said. 'I'll show you how we lived together,' but I knew, even as I was saying it, that she wouldn't be able to see what I meant in the walls or the blue shutters or the earth-coloured tiles on the floor, but she might understand the feeling because she'd said that she couldn't describe what it was like for her where she grew up.

We gazed at the water that seemed to keep coming from over the horizon. The blue filled my eyes and I tasted the salt on my tongue, feeling the depth and endless reach of the sea. Sandy had his proud nose up, pointed in the direction we were going, his ears flapping, his feathery fur light and golden in the sun, looking for where he belonged too. I wasn't entirely sure what Beth was hoping to find or why she felt she needed to come with us, but I liked the feeling of having her there with me anyway.

The shape of Chelona island grew before our eyes, as if we had stayed still the whole time and it had floated towards us. Grandfather had once told me about the colony of nesting turtles that laid their eggs there, and about the people who protected them so the turtles could nest in peace. Sometimes people visited Chelona for the beaches and the water sports and diving, but every other year there were special trips to see the turtles hatching at night. You just had to be lucky enough to be in the right place at the right time to see them. The turtle that had come to our island now and two years ago was unusual because we'd not had one nesting there before. Maybe that one turtle had gone off course, or maybe Chelona had become too crowded because of all the other turtles.

I imagined Grandfather quietly keeping an eye on the comings and goings of turtles in a secluded cove on Chelona, and how in that quiet watching he would learn everything there was to know about turtles. There would be so many things that he could tell me, that I'd want him to share only with me. And then I didn't want to imagine any more. Had he already seen turtle eggs hatching? Had he watched with wonder without me there?

16

The lost-property office on Chelona was muggy and musty, full of shelves piled with unclaimed lost black suitcases and strappy backpacks. Beth did all the talking while I stayed in the doorway, scanning the quay with Sandy next to me. Sandy was staring out at the ferry, which was still tied to the bollards on the quayside while passengers boarded to go on to another island further away. I looked at every bench and boat, hoping to see a man with a blue cap and walking stick. I looked over at the tavernas where old men sat in the shade on raffia chairs at tables with paper tablecloths, sipping from small coffee cups and playing dominoes. I couldn't see Grandfather among them.

'Azi!' Beth said sharply, and I realised she might have called my name a few times. A teenage boy was leaning across the counter, chewing gum. I went over and Sandy followed. The teenager said he sometimes remembered who got on the boats – he had nothing much to do all day but stare out of the door at the quay – and he wanted to know which day I'd found the dog. I explained that the dog found *me*, which made Beth sigh.

'It was Monday a couple of weeks ago,' I said.

The teenager stretched the gum with his tongue.

'Nope. Don't remember any dogs on that Monday,' he said.

'He might have come over the night before – on the Sunday,' I said.

'Good point,' the teenager said, then he seemed to go off in a dream.

After a while, Beth asked him if he was thinking about who he remembered getting on the boat on the Sunday but he just shrugged and asked if there was anything else we wanted.

'Something helpful would be nice,' Beth said, sounding fed up. 'Have you got a form we can fill in?' she said, and we did that quickly because I was eager to get outside and look around.

Beth was very disappointed with the lost-property boy but thought walking around would be a good idea so we could ask people if they recognised Sandy. But the old men in the tavernas round the quay didn't know Grandfather and didn't know the dog either. Beth went into shops and I took the opportunity to ask the old men where I could find Andreas. They told me he was out fishing. Grandfather had said a fisherman didn't need a watch – the time he spent out at sea depended on the catch, not the clock. The sea gave him its own feelings of what was enough for today and it was never the same. Tides, currents, swells, calms, the hot days and cooler days, all had their own feel for how long to stay out at sea. So I knew I'd be lucky to find Andreas before the ferry took us back.

Beth, Sandy and I went from one end of the quay to the other several times.

'What shall we do now?' Beth said.

I'd thought about exactly how I wanted things to go when we came to Chelona. We'd see Andreas, he'd point to a cottage at the end of the quay and there would be Grandfather, sitting on a bench, his eyes shaded by a blue cap, squinting into the sun to see who was running to meet him. I'd tell him I was sorry and he'd just come home. The reality wasn't turning out to be like that at all. It was frustrating being on the quay when nothing we wanted to find seemed to be there.

'What do turtles remind you of when you think about them?' I asked Beth.

She could only think of the story of the hare and the tortoise, saying the moral of that story was that you had to be patient. But I'd already been patient for two years. How much longer did I have to wait? Did it mean that Grandfather wasn't ready to forgive me yet? Or ever?

'I'm getting hot,' Beth said. 'There's a museum over there, let's go inside.'

The museum displayed ancient Greek artefacts,

sections of pillars, pottery bowls, wine jars and oil jars. Beth stared into the glass cases, pointing out things that would be good to build a newly imagined perfect place. I hardly saw what was there, keeping a lookout through the doorway whenever I could in case Grandfather walked by, but only seeing Sandy sitting there staring back at me inside.

'Azi! Come and look at this,' Beth said.

She had found an ancient statue of pale marble of the goddess Aphrodite. She read the information card. Aphrodite was the symbol of love and beauty but it wasn't her that Beth was pointing at. Under Aphrodite's foot was a turtle. Beth kept reading, leaving her finger on a word to say what the turtle meant, but I didn't understand.

'I think that word means that you will have lots of babies,' she said. 'Does that help?'

It didn't.

'Turtle shells are kind of like shields,' I said, thinking aloud. Perhaps Grandfather needed me to protect him in some way, or maybe it meant I should have protected him more. 'Let's go and find the nesting site,' I said, leaving the museum, Sandy immediately following and Beth running to catch up.

The nesting site wasn't signposted, but I knew the lie of Chelona from maps and stories Grandfather had told me. From higher up on a sun-baked hill looking out to sea it didn't take me long to work out on which currents the turtles might have come. We walked for half an hour, Beth sheltering under the shade of a tree whenever we came across one, until finally we came to a quiet cove away from the tourist beaches, fenced off and with signs saying to keep out. There were other telltale signs that this was the nesting site: the fact that there were hardly any human footprints, the mounds in the sand, and also that the beach was completely cleared of litter.

Beth said she was exhausted. Her cheeks were red, her forehead sweaty, so I found her a cool place facing the breeze under the shade of some trees. I gave her drinks and food from the backpack and we ate our lunch. Beth wondered what time it was. I noticed she wasn't wearing a watch either and the white patch on her skin where it had been before was turning pink.

'I forgot to take my watch off when I went swimming in the sea and it doesn't work any more,' she said.

I guessed it was about two o'clock, feeling frustrated that we didn't have much time left, and that I hadn't found what I was looking for. I tried to climb on the wire fence.

'Azi, we're not allowed in there!' Beth said. 'And your uncle said we should stay at the quay.'

'She's right, you're not allowed in there,' came a man's voice.

Two men and a lady had arrived, all wearing yellow turtle-conservation T-shirts and caps. 'And don't let the dog in either; it might dig up the nests.'

Beth looked flustered but I didn't want to go back without something that told me I was getting nearer to finding Grandfather.

'I just wanted to see them,' I said. 'I wouldn't do anything to hurt the turtles and neither would Sandy. And I know where there's another nest,' I said, stalling.

'*I've* seen the nest too,' Beth said, sounding bothered and fed up again.

They wanted to know more so we stayed talking with them for a while. I told them everything I knew about the one turtle with the chipped shell on our island. They all shared a look between each other, commenting that they were really pleased to have this new information. I asked them about turtles; what did they mean?

The woman told me that in historic cultures turtles signified wisdom and patience. Turtles were gentle and calm, like old souls of the sea, and that's why she loved them.

'They represent time, don't they?' said the other man.

'Azi!' Beth said, tipping her head to read the woman's watch. 'The ferry goes in fifteen minutes!'

'Time you were leaving,' the man said. 'You mustn't tell anyone that you found this place because if too many people come here, the turtles won't.'

We assured them we wouldn't and I gave them

some flyers and told them to visit Uncle's restaurant on our island and then we ran.

Beth found it hard in the searing heat, stopping to bend over with her head down and her hands on her knees. Sandy trotted along between us, looking back at Beth, forward at me. I had to keep going. I didn't want to miss seeing Andreas if he was there. Beth was more worried about us missing the ferry than seeing Andreas, about her parents and Uncle being cross too. As I came over the hill I saw the ferry waiting at the quay, people boarding. Beth was still a long way behind me. Sandy was stuck in the middle of us, not sure who to be with. Alongside the ferry there was a small fishing boat, and a man with thick black hair was throwing lobster pots on to the quay.

'Andreas!' I yelled as I ran, hoping it was him, kicking off my flip-flops and leaving them behind so I was able to run faster.

The man looked up and I ran over. It was Andreas.

'Have you seen Evander Marinos?' I asked him.

'Evander? No.' He rested his elbow on his knee on the side of the boat. 'I heard he'd lost his boat, though.' He nodded out to sea. 'I used to pass him sometimes out there but I haven't seen him for a couple of years.'

My heart sank.

The ferry crew were waiting to pull up the gang-plank and unhook the ropes. Beth was nearly here and I could see how worried she looked that the ferry might leave without us. The ferry engine started and I told her to go and get on board, to take Sandy with her, I'd be there in a minute.

'Have you heard anything about him?' I asked Andreas.

Andreas then called across the quay to the old

fellows still sitting outside the taverna, asking them if there was any talk of Evander Marinos. They slowly shook their heads. They were the same men I'd already asked.

'If you hear from him or about him, could you tell him . . .' I faltered. What message could I leave?

'Azi!' Beth was shouting from the boat, hanging on to Sandy, the crew around her also calling me to hurry.

I kneeled down and sloshed the tin bucket in the sea, pulling seaweed and mussel shells from the quayside wall. I balanced the bucket on the rocks nearby at the edge of the sea.

'Evander is my grandfather,' I called back to Andreas. 'Tell him Azi left this bucket. Tell him he has to pour it into the sea. He'll know what it means,' and then I ran, leaping on to the ferry as the engines churned the water and it moved away.

Beth said the sun was blinding her when she wiped her eyes after I was safely on board the ferry and the crew had told me off.

'Now you've lost your bucket,' Beth said miserably, 'and we had to carry your shoes.'

Beth had one, Sandy had the other in his mouth.

'And I don't suppose you even asked that fisherman if he knew Sandy.'

I kept quiet when she sat at the other end of the bench seat. After a while she shuffled over and asked if I really meant to find Sandy's home or was the dog only an excuse to find Grandfather.

'I want you to be the first to succeed in building your Atlantis,' she said. She crouched down and put her arms round Sandy. 'But I want to see Sandy go home as well. Most of all, I wanted us to find all these things *together*.'

'Sorry,' I said, because I could see now why I kept upsetting her. I was leaving her out.

She said I could share anything with her, that she was on my side. She asked, was I on her side? 'Sometimes I think you've got a whole big story about everything we're doing,' she said. 'But you're keeping it all to yourself.'

There were no problems I told Maria that night out the back of the restaurant. None at all. No, nothing.

'Hmm,' she said. 'Either my cousin is a terrible fibber, or you are.'

'She's not,' I said, hanging my head, telling her how Beth and I hadn't had a watch, how we didn't find Andreas until the last minute. 'It won't happen again.'

'I know it won't,' she said, tucking my hair round

157

my ear. 'Grandfather didn't raise you to tell lies, did he?'

She asked about Beth and Sandy too, and I thought even more about how Beth wanted to be included, that *we* were all looking for a place to belong and that Beth wouldn't find her belonging, not here, not yet.

'The dog's owner wasn't on Chelona then?' Maria said.

I shook my head.

'Keep looking. He's out there somewhere.'

Grandfather said it was all out there. The sea told a story about all of us – where we came from and where all the answers were. Even monsters from the deep were part of a much bigger story.

But what did all that mean?

17

Beth came to see me early the next morning and told me her family had come to the island on their own boat and they were going sailing so she wouldn't be able to help with our search for a few days. Their boat was moored at the marina and she was on her way there now. She hadn't come to this island on a ferry and when I asked her how come I'd found her passport at the quay, she said that she'd had it in her pocket, that she was looking around and must have dropped it. She asked me not to go to any of the islands without her. I promised I wouldn't.

'What were you looking for at the quay?' I said.

'Nothing really,' she said. She spun on the sand. 'I was wondering if I was brave enough to get on a ferry all by myself and I thought I needed a passport, but it turns out that I didn't.'

'Why were you going to catch a ferry?'

She looked down at the ground and then back up. 'I didn't need to,' she said and grinned. 'I saw you pick up my passport.'

She left me baffled. Why hadn't she come over and asked me to give it back straight away?

I had two days with Sandy to dive and swim, and work out which island we'd visit next. I dived to the wreck of Grandfather's fishing boat, hoping

I'd see something that would tell me which of all the islands he was living on. Maybe Delos, maybe Skia? Which one?

I went back to the cottage, back to the place where everything made sense. Even though Grandfather wasn't there, our memories were, and although they'd remind me of who was missing, they also might help me find him.

'I need to think like Grandfather,' I told Sandy. The turtle, the door, the passport – what did all the three signs mean? Surely one of them would lead me to the right island and to him.

I sat in Grandfather's chair while Sandy sat on the rug at my feet. In those last months before Grandfather left, I'd look up from my bed over the other side of the room during the night to see him sitting here in his chair, his shawl round his shoulders, his bottle beside him, mumbling in his dreams.

And then the beast from the deep would rise up, making him call out and cry.

'Grandfather? Are you okay?' I'd whisper.

'Who's that?' he'd say, his fingers stiff and cracked like driftwood, closing like instinct round the tipping glass. His eyes had seemed to be turned inwards, to some black depth that only he could see through the fog of the grog.

'It's me, Azi.'

Lost in the mist of waterlogged memories, it would take a moment for him to find me in the puddle of the moon in the dark of the room. Then he'd smile and take a sip to soften his brittle waking up.

'Azi, I found you. My pearl from the sea,' he'd say with a sigh. Saltwater would overflow from his eyes at the joy he seemed to find in me, in the same way it did for me when he told me who I was to him. Under the sway of the grog, the line blurred between story and history but that hadn't mattered to me. As long as the story was ours, as long as we were in it, as long as it was shared between us. Then I'd go and sit beside him and he'd touch my head, touch my feet, as if making sure I was really there.

Sandy rested his chin on my knee at that moment. I looked at that dog as Grandfather must have looked at me. I couldn't believe for one moment that Grandfather didn't want to come back to where he belonged.

Then somebody knocked at the front door.

'Mr Marinos, are you in there? It's Nick from the developers.'

I'd left the door off the latch and as I got up to go over it swung open, the man still knocking. He must have assumed Grandfather was inside. The man was wearing a blue shirt, stone-coloured trousers and proper shiny shoes; his hair was neat and he carried a leather wallet under his arm.

'I brought the papers . . . Oh, I'm looking for Evander Marinos,' he said.

So was I.

'I'm Azi,' I said. 'He's my grandfather.' All sorts of things swam in my head as this man stood by the open blue front door.

'I was hoping to find him here, Azi. He phoned the office yesterday but didn't leave a phone number or address. When you see him would you give him my personal contact details and tell him to get in touch again?'

He pressed a small white card in my hand. *Papadopoulos Property Developers.* My mind was going mad. The shaking began inside me. *Grandfather had spoken to this man only yesterday.*

'Why does he need to speak to you?' I said, the words racing out of my mouth.

'He's selling us his cottage but he needs to sign the papers.' Nick stepped forward as I stepped back, shaking my head again and again. 'Azi? Are you all right?' he said, crouching down beside me as I fell back into Grandfather's chair. Sandy whined and hid behind the chair.

'He can't sell the cottage,' I said. 'He's coming back to live here.'

Nick was quiet for a moment and then he spoke calmly. He told me that his company planned to build a hotel. They had already bought the cottages either side of Grandfather's, and the land they were on. Grandfather's cottage in the middle of the row was all that stood in his way. It was business. They'd been planning the project for years and were now ready to start. Grandfather only needed to sign.

In that moment Nick took away every scrap of hope that I had. It wasn't a question any more of me finding Grandfather, of me telling him I was sorry and that I would never fight with him again, that I would never have told Uncle about the grog. Now it seemed as if the signs meant that Grandfather *didn't* want to come home after all.

'This is where he belongs. This is where *I* belong,' I said. 'You've made a mistake.'

'I grew up here on this island too,' Nick said, going on to tell me that he lived on the mainland now. He said he knew what it meant to belong to a place and he came back time and time again to visit. 'I want to do something for the people who live here now, though,' he explained. 'Building a hotel will help bring more tourists. All the businesses here need more trade to survive.'

He said he understood how I felt. He still had memories, a history, a story he could share with his family of where his roots were and that was what mattered to him, not the stone and mortar. He wasn't trying to tear down our community but trying to build it up and make it better. I told him Beth's idea about Atlantis and he smiled. 'Yes, kind of like that,' he said.

'If your grandfather is having trouble finding somewhere else to live . . .' Nick trailed off, saying he could see it wasn't what it was about for me. He'd have to wait for Grandfather to call him back, or I was to let him know if I found Grandfather. He got up, telling me to hold on to his card, that he'd help me and Grandfather in any way he could.

'Time is a good healer,' he said.

But even a whole jar of honey couldn't heal the

hurt I felt inside. Only Grandfather coming home would do that.

Two more islands. I would have to find Grandfather before Nick did.

18

'WHERE ARE WE GOING THIS TIME?' BETH SAID, freshly back from sailing with her parents, with stories of a lost ancient city underwater where her father had taken her diving. She left the choice to me and was excited, chatting to Maria, trying to guess which island I had chosen.

The second sign had to be the door. And because of the door, I'd found out more of the bigger story.

'This island is small and has a famous door,' I said.

Maria knew where I meant but Beth had never heard of a door being famous. She had a guidebook and flicked through it, muttering – 'No, no, wait, don't tell me. I'm still trying to guess.' – eventually holding up a picture and saying, 'Thyra!'

We bought our tickets. I asked Maria if there was anyone she knew that we could ask about finding Grandfather. 'Leda,' she said, twitching her mouth. She told us that we'd find her at one of the souvenir kiosks, and that she might be able to help, or she might not. 'Ask her anyway,' she said.

Beth was wearing a hat and her watch today. She said her watch hadn't broken after all and then admitted she'd taken it off because I didn't wear one, and she wanted to be the same as me. She had some funny ideas. I thought of me and

Grandfather, how different we looked on the outside, but how we were the same on the inside.

We boarded the ferry, breathing the air as it took us across the sea, feeling the breeze cool what the sun heated up, Sandy sitting like a figurehead at the front with his nose held high.

'You're even quieter than normal,' Beth said. 'What's up?'

'Nothing,' I said. I didn't want to share the news about the cottage with anyone.

Thyra was a very small island and there was no lost-property office there. So what happened to things that got lost or found? And who were we going to leave details of Sandy with? Beth said we'd have to tell as many people as we could in the shops and the tavernas along the quay, that we'd widen our search, asking everyone we met. The more people we told, the more chance they would tell someone else, until eventually news might reach Sandy's owner. At the same time we would ask about Grandfather.

Waiters in white shirts holding trays of cold drinks above their shoulders stopped to look at Sandy and shake their head. Young fishermen didn't know Evander Marinos and they'd not seen the dog before. I wanted to keep moving, to find something more.

We found Leda fanning herself under a big sun umbrella outside the door of her souvenir shop. When Maria had said that she wasn't sure if Leda could help us, I thought it would be because Leda might be a bit like Mrs Halimeda. But Leda was very friendly and opened some fold-up chairs for us to sit on, saying she was sure she could help us. She thought Beth ought to sit in the shade, though, because she was much more pale-skinned than me and it was hot. Beth struggled with the heat as the day baked. Leda gave us cans of ice-cold drink and waved away our money when we offered to pay.

'Yes, I think I have seen this dog before; he looks familiar,' she said, as Sandy sat at her feet, wagging his tail while she fed him ice cubes.

'Really?' Beth said, asking when, where, who was he with?

Leda didn't answer at first but had a long story to tell us about a dog that belonged to her when she was a girl. He was like Sandy, very much like Sandy. A story from the past.

Beth glanced over at me, frowning. 'But what about *this* dog?' Beth asked Leda.

'Maybe I'm remembering the dog that belonged to me,' Leda murmured. 'No, I don't think I know this one.'

There was something about Leda's misted eyes

that reminded me of Grandfather when the grog had taken him into the past.

'And Evander Marinos?' I said, hopeful. 'He was a fisherman. Do you know him?'

'Evander Marinos? No, I'm not sure now . . .' She fanned herself and then clapped her hands together. 'Yes, of course, Evander!'

Hope stirred in me but Beth took her hat off, wiped her forehead, put her hat back on and huffed, rolling her eyes. We listened to another long, long story of Leda's days as a young woman and her sweetheart, Evander, who was a sailor in the Navy with a beautiful uniform, and how he'd swept her off her feet. Beth made a face at Leda's gushing.

'But he wasn't in the Navy,' I said. 'He was a fisherman.'

'A man of the sea, what difference does it make? Evander, yes that was his name,' Leda said. 'No, not Evander . . . Georgiou. Yes, Georgiou! Such a handsome man. My heart belonged to Georgiou. I wonder what happened to him?'

We left Leda, who had invited us back whenever we wanted. I said this ought to be called the island of memories, but Beth said it should be called the island of forgetfulness. She said Leda had been leading us up the garden path. I agreed with her on that, but said I didn't think she'd meant to. Leda seemed lonely. Why else would she ask us to sit and talk of all the things that brought her closer to her beloved dog and sweetheart?

'Look at Sandy,' Beth said. Sandy was long and thin anyway but now seemed slumped and deflated. 'Don't you think his nose would find where he belonged if it was nearby?'

'If only we had one of his owner's socks . . .' I started to say. 'What if I brought one of Grandfather's socks with us? Maybe Sandy could sniff him out?'

Beth sighed with me. We wished we'd thought of it before we'd gone to either of the islands. We'd been looking for Sandy's owner the best way we could, but Sandy might be much better at finding him than we were.

The heat was making Beth cranky and she marched on, following a sign that pointed to the famous doorway of Thyra.

We walked on, up a steep stony path to the top of a cliff. Ahead of us was the entrance to the ancient temple that had long ago been destroyed and crumbled to almost nothing. All that was still standing was the two stone pillars, about four times as high as us, and as wide as Beth and I with our arms stretched out and touching hands. Across the top there was a stone beam with a frieze carved into it, worn by the wind and salt and sun. As we stood in the doorway the view of the deep blue sea sparkling below and all around took our breath away.

Nobody else was there to ask if they knew Grandfather or Sandy. The sun was high and Beth and I sat with our backs against the pillars, Beth lying at the small angle of the shade it cast. Sandy was sniffing, as if he'd found a trail invisible to us.

'This is the most amazing doorway I have ever seen in my whole life,' Beth said.

The door wasn't actually there so Beth wanted us to imagine what it looked like, what it was made of – wood? Or gold? – and how many people it took to swing it open.

'You can tell that when you opened it there must have been something amazing to go into,' she said. 'A place like Atlantis probably.'

'Buildings always seem to end up falling down,

being blown to bits in wars or being pulled down,' I said, wondering what had happened to all the people who used to live here. 'Everything seems like it's made of sand.'

Sandy had come to the end of his trail now. He'd found an ice cream that an earlier visitor had dropped and licked at the sticky puddle on the ground.

Before we knew it, time had run out. We returned to Leda's so I could buy a bucket.

'I remember you two,' Leda said. 'You were looking for Georgiou.' We smiled at her.

'Loneliness is a terrible thing,' Beth said to me.

I filled the bucket with seawater and made a mini aquarium before balancing it on the rocks that ran out into the sea by the quay. There was nobody to ask to point it out to Grandfather if he came there. He would know it was from me and what it meant, though.

I was badly disappointed that Thyra hadn't given us any clues as to where Grandfather was. I wasn't sure now what the door could have meant as a sign – was it simply to tell me that Grandfather's house was being demolished? That I'd have no home with him? Thyra was one more island that Grandfather almost definitely wasn't living on, but that didn't mean I was getting any closer to finding the one he was. And it was the same for Sandy too. There was hardly anyone on the ferry home and Sandy sat on his own on the bench at the stern, looking back to where we had come from.

Our last trip to an island had to be to the right one. The third sign was Beth's passport.

19

The last island visit was more important than ever. Beth and I thought and thought about how we might choose one, while I was still wondering what it might have to do with Beth's passport. In the meantime, I'd collected Grandfather's sock from his cottage and given it to Sandy to sniff to see if he could follow the scent in case it could help us. We couldn't be sure exactly if Sandy would be able to do it and we knew he wouldn't be able to sniff Grandfather out from here, but we wouldn't know if we didn't try. And if we did go to an island and it was the wrong island, we'd have wasted our last journey anyway.

A dog must have good memories of smells because when I let Sandy sniff the sock, he led Beth and I through the narrow streets. He was heading in the direction of Grandfather's cottage, but it might just have been because he had been there before. As we followed him I was telling Beth some good memories of Grandfather and me fishing and diving, but as we got near to the cottage I saw lots of people I knew, and didn't know, standing in the road. Mrs Halimeda, Maria, passing tourists and men from the property developers in high-visibility tunics. Wired fences were all around the whole row of cottages, a bulldozer and diggers rumbling where the two cottages had already been demolished.

Had Grandfather signed the papers? I pushed past everyone, anger rising in me at Nick the developer not telling me that he had found Grandfather. I ran at the fence and tried to climb, to stop them from pulling Grandfather's cottage down. The long heavy arm of the digger swung out, crashing into the blue front door.

'Stop! NO!' I yelled. 'That's my home!'

'Whoa there, young man,' one of the builders said, his arms catching me round my waist and pulling me down off the fence.

'Where's Nick?' I shouted. 'Why didn't he tell me?'

In that moment all that had begun to undo between Grandfather and me two years ago unravelled completely as I kicked out. Mrs Halimeda shook her head at me, as if she was satisfied that being raised by Grandfather had come to this, that my behaviour was all Grandfather's doing.

'You can't knock it down!' I shouted, trying to pull the man's strong arms off as he held me to his chest, pinning me down. 'Someone must have made him sign. The grog made him sign. He wouldn't have meant to!'

'I'm sure it's not what you think,' Maria said, running over, telling the man to put me down, that she'd take care of me.

'Too much grog always ends in disaster,' Mrs Halimeda muttered. 'He was no good for anything!'

'He was the best! You don't know anything!' I shouted as Maria held on to my arms. 'Grandfather was everything – to me!'

I pulled free and ran from them, all the way back to the cove. Beth and Sandy arrived shortly after but stayed quietly at a distance and let me be angry, let me spit and scream and pant and kick the sand and throw stones. And when some of the rage had gone out of me and I was sitting under the shadow of the door with my head in my hands Beth and Sandy came over and sat down too.

'I was right about Atlantis and I'm right about all perfect places. I knew how it would turn out. It's all doomed to crumble into ruins,' I said through my teeth.

'You can rebuild a new place, even from ruins,' Beth said quietly, the dog tucked in close beside her as she scraped sand into a pile, patting it smooth.

'You can't build places by talking about them!'

'It's not just talk,' she said. 'We really did make a start with all the things we imagined, and we can keep doing it.'

'You don't understand!' I said. 'He *can't* come back now!'

The day before Grandfather left, when I had asked him why the boys at school said I didn't belong here, he'd said he wasn't my grandfather, he wasn't a father to my parents, and Uncle wasn't my uncle. I wasn't sure if it had been the grog or the truth talking. I wondered if he had actually told me that before – when I was small, crawling on my hands and knees, only speaking a few words, and that somehow it had always been there in my memory, something deep and buried that I kind of already knew. Had we only pretended we were Grandfather and Azi, like a play – a story about us; a tall fisherman's tale that had come to an end? I had been happy that even if it had just been a story we were still those people who had lived together with those names.

While the grog had pickled Grandfather's memories, he had said other things too. He had told me that my parents had died in a war. That I had been born without a home.

Grandfather's drinking had made his body weak and his mind feeble. He had drowned in his own sorrows but what else lurked in the deep? Did it even matter when we had made a perfect place for the both of us? An old man and a creature from the sea. How could he give all this up when I was sure it had meant as much to him as it had to me?

Beth was collecting stones and shells from the beach as these thoughts ran through my head, laying them in lines leading off from the propped-up door that I was sitting beside.

'You can share your feelings with me,' she said, as she laid the stones one at a time in another line. But the anger wouldn't subside. Adrift, I couldn't find anything to hold on to.

'What are you doing?' I snapped.

'I'm marking out a home for you,' she said. She spread her arms. 'The cornerstone could be here.' She jumped up to show the height of the walls, and ran straight lines round the sides of the building that she saw in her imagination, making it sound like the possibility of the walls of a house I could live in.

'Just stop,' I said.

She piled up some more sand. 'You could have a palm tree here, and when it's grown it will cast a shade so you can sit outside in the cool.' She marked the shadow of the palm tree, scraping her foot along the sand to expose the darker wet sand underneath. 'From here, you could watch over the turtles and always be right by the sea.'

'No!' I yelled. 'Stop it!' None of this meant anything without Grandfather.

Beth let the handful of sand fall from between her fingers. 'Sometimes you go into your shell like a hermit crab, Azi.'

'I'm not a creature!' I said, hurt and angry. 'I'm not turtle boy, or sea boy or aqua boy!' I shouted.

'I never said you were.' Her lips trembled. 'You didn't understand what I was trying to do, did you?'

'You're a tourist!'

'*Nomad!*' she said quite strongly. 'My family are *global* nomads!'

She wiped the sand from her hands and walked away. I was too angry to apologise, too hurt to be sorry about how much I must have hurt her.

I stormed off and telephoned Nick from the phone box. I called him a liar.

'Azi, listen to me,' came the voice from the other end of the line, but I didn't want to.

'You promised!' I yelled until I couldn't yell any more.

Grandfather hadn't taught me to be like this. But I couldn't stop the hurt making me do it.

Nick told me that he wasn't on our island and that the site manager had gone ahead with the building work without telling him. He hadn't even heard that the paperwork had been signed. He was sorry that things had happened like this. So where was Grandfather? Nick was over on the mainland but he said he'd call the office to find out what they knew. He promised me again, told me he was on my side, that he understood how attached to the cottage I was and that he would help in any way he could, but he also had many other people to consider.

'Azi, are you still there?' he said, asking how he could get in touch with me.

Then as the tide of anger died in me, leaving me tired, lonely and feeling guilty about how horrible I'd been, Nick asked me to tell him more about Grandfather. What was he like? And so I told him the story of Grandfather the fisherman sailing the boiling seas, the monsters he wrestled, the fish he caught. And I told him how we had lived together, and how the cove had been our place. I told him how much I missed being with Grandfather, and how he had to come back soon to see the turtles hatch.

'My promise still stands,' Nick said finally. 'I'll be in touch.'

I couldn't let him call Uncle's, so I gave him Maria's phone number instead.

20

THE COVE WAS THE ONLY PLACE I WANTED TO BE.
Wrapped in the curve of the rocks at either end,
I sat under the shade of the door and then swam,
diving deep to where the noise was gone, where
the cool washed the heat out of me. I thought
again of the last time I had been really angry with
Grandfather, the day before he left, when the bottle
broke apart as well as our life together. It was all

my fault. I should have left things as they were. Sandy came to the beach for a while and then disappeared and I didn't see Beth, but I wouldn't have gone to the third island without her anyway. After a few days I was missing her too.

I went looking for Beth and found her sitting on the quayside, Sandy beside her. I sat down next to her and said sorry, what I needed to say to Grandfather too. I didn't mean any of the horrible things that I'd said. I wanted her to come with me. I wanted her to help me. I wanted us to be friends. I was uncomfortable sharing my feelings but I said them anyway, because that's what she'd wanted all along.

'I'm homesick and lonely without Grandfather and it hurts, and then I get angry and I forget to think about anyone else.' It made me think of Uncle, how for the last two years he had kept me going by telling me to think about the customers.

'Thanks,' she said. 'I can tell you mean it.' And I did.

She was quiet for a minute, much quieter than she usually was, and I hoped everything really was okay with us.

'I need to feel like a warrior today,' she said after a while. 'I need to protect myself both from the outside and the inside of our perfect place.'

'Our perfect place?' I said, but I didn't want to argue with her and was curious as to what she meant.

'It's a place I thought us three made for a while.' She touched Sandy's head and he half closed his eyes, enjoying the scratch.

I was beginning to understand what Beth meant and I *was* happier being with them, having both of them for company, knowing I had her on my side, that she understood the homesickness, the feeling of not belonging. She held up a bag from the pharmacy store and showed me what was inside. A box of blue hair dye.

'I'm going to have a warrior hairstyle because if I look strong on the outside, it will help me feel strong on the inside,' she said. I saw something sad in her watery eyes. 'Sandy's owner called my mum and he's coming over on a ferry this afternoon to take Sandy home.'

I wasn't ready, and felt breathless, as if I was underwater, fighting to find the surface. Leda *had* recognised Sandy after all, found his owner and called the number we had left with her. Sandy belonged to a Mr Tassi who lived over the other side of Thyra. The dog that sometimes reminded me of Grandfather, who quietly and gently hung around us like a friendly shadow, was suddenly much more than a stray dog now I knew it was the last time he'd be with us. Beth was right, all three of us had found a perfect place with each other for a while, and now it was almost over. All the memories of Grandfather leaving swamped me, but I also knew that this was what we had hoped for Sandy all along.

'We'll be stronger together,' I said. 'Come with me.' We ran through the streets, preparing for the battle that was coming inside ourselves. I knocked on Maria's door again and again until she opened it.

'I need a warrior haircut,' I said.

We told Maria that Sandy was going home. Beth's hair was really short anyway and didn't need cutting and, when Maria asked, Beth said her parents were fine with her colouring it. She told us her mum used to dye her hair different colours all the time and understood what she was doing. Maria let Beth dye her hair over the sink with a towel round her shoulders. In the meantime Maria gave me news. Nick had called that morning with a message for me to say that Grandfather had visited the office at the mainland, but not when Nick was there. He had signed the papers and left on a ferry, but Nick didn't know where he had gone. Grandfather had given Uncle's address at the restaurant for the paperwork.

And while I tried not to think about the fact that maybe Grandfather didn't want me to find him, Beth came back from rinsing her hair in the bathroom. She looked like some kind of creature from the sea with her watery blue-green eyes and her hair dyed sea-blue. It seemed to mean something to her to have hair that colour, as if she could be someone else for a while, connected to something mighty like the sea that could help bear the battle coming.

'You look like a mermaid,' I said, and Beth smiled.

Maria washed my hair, then dragged a comb through tangles I didn't know had knotted themselves there. Beth tried some hairstyles on me, pulling my hair back in a ponytail, rolling it like a knot on the top of my head, making a long fringe over my face, and we started laughing at how many different types of people I looked like, what names I would have.

'I want my hair like a sea urchin,' I said, 'because they have spines to protect themselves.'

And then we laughed, as if it was the funniest thing in the world, while Maria clipped the sides of my hair really short and left the top longer and spiked it up. Beth gelled her hair all spiky too.

'You look invincible,' Beth said to me.

'He looks like the real Samson,' Maria said.

Beth and I stood, side by side, looking at ourselves in the mirror. Sandy sat and stared up at us. He seemed to be smiling too.

We took Sandy to the cove before the ferry came and leaped up with him, as if to reach the seagulls hovering over our heads, singing with him a dog's song of joy, even when the birds flew out of our reach. Then we lay down, trying to hold on to the warm, dry sand in our hands as it slowly trickled through our fingers.

21

Bᴇᴛʜ ᴀɴᴅ I sᴛᴏᴏᴅ ᴏɴ ᴛʜᴇ ǫᴜᴀʏsɪᴅᴇ ᴡɪᴛʜ Sᴀɴᴅʏ, our warrior haircuts and fiercely brave hearts facing the sea. As a last attempt to use Sandy's nose to find Grandfather I let him sniff Grandfather's sock, which I had in my pocket, and showed him the timetable.

'Can you tell me where he is, Sandy? Somewhere out there?'

Sandy sniffed and then looked up at me. His long, hairy tail wagged slowly. Then he sat down on my feet and turned his head to look out, still devoted to watching the sea while the ferry rumbled in. Beth and I had been trying to find his home, but now that we had found it we were trying to hold on to Sandy a little longer. We wanted to be sure that Mr Tassi really was Sandy's owner – that Sandy knew him, loved him and wanted to go home with him. After all of the passengers had come ashore there was hardly anyone left – certainly no one who seemed to be a man looking for a dog. We began to wonder if Mr Tassi had come at all.

'He could have been held up by an emergency,' Beth said.

A small part of me was glad that Sandy might have to stay, even just for another day or two; a huge part of me knew what had to be.

'We don't even know what Mr Tassi looks like,' I said, gazing out along the quay to where an old man was pushing an old lady in a wheelchair. They were heading for the lost-property office, which was closed. It had to be them. We agreed it might be Mr *and* Mrs Tassi but we weren't sure how good a dog's eyesight was as Sandy hadn't noticed them at all. Dogs were better at using their noses and ears. I threw some scraps further and further along the quayside so Sandy would go and get them. For a minute he kept coming back to us until we all heard Mr Tassi's voice, quaking and trembling.

'Is that him over there. Is that our boy?'

'Is it?' said his wife. 'Is it, love? Oh, it is! I can't believe it, after all this time.'

Sandy's slow recognition of their voices started in the pricking of his ears, a purposeful step, his eyes brightening, his nose twitching and glistening, and then he suddenly galloped across the quay. He didn't leap at them, as if he knew the unsteadiness of their age. Instead, he swayed at their feet, his tail wagging and wagging, then he whined and licked them and rolled over. Mr Tassi and his wife laughed and cried, gathering the dog into themselves.

'He looks so different with them, so alive,' Beth said, as we shared his joy at finding his owners again, and then we felt the pain of trying to hold on to him and leaned into each other. We were losing our friend, but at least we had each other.

'I feel a part of that dog, even though we're over here,' I said.

'Here we all are,' said Mr Tassi, his arm round his wife and Sandy, kissing them each in turn.

'Give him the treats, hurry now,' Mrs Tassi said,

reaching for the bag strung over the back of her wheelchair. 'There's a good boy, Fílos.'

And then he wasn't our Sand Dog any more. His name was Fílos. Friend. But we would always remember him as Sandy.

Sandy walked beside the wheelchair, Mr Tassi letting go with one hand every few steps to stroke his dog. The dog's long, stiff stride, now eased with joy, suddenly looked completely right as he walked beside the slowly rolling wheelchair, pushed by an elderly man walking with the same slow, stiff stride. Beth and I moved closer, to see and hear what it was like to be back with who you belonged to, to share a small part of it.

'We should stop for some refreshments before we head back,' Mrs Tassi said to her husband. 'We'll buy Fílos an ice cream. You know he loves ice cream.'

Mr Tassi nodded. 'We've got an hour before the ferry home. We've just got time.'

'Let's sit over in the shade. Is there a water bowl there for Fílos?' his wife said, giving him a dish from her bag. 'Here, take this and ask them to fill it up.'

Mr Tassi stopped pushing for a moment, looking around.

'What is it?' Mrs Tassi asked.

'I'm wondering,' Mr Tassi said. 'Who's been looking after him all this time? He looks well, doesn't he? I don't think he's been too lonely.'

Beth and I held our breaths. Although we wanted to go and tell them all about us, what we had shared and to say goodbye, something stopped us both. I turned to look at Beth.

'We have to let him go completely,' Beth whispered. We didn't make a move to tell them who we were, who Sandy had been to us, because of how completely happy Sandy was to be back with them.

We had an hour before the ferry left to decide whether we'd be able to wave goodbye. After Mr and Mrs Tassi had gone to the refreshment kiosk, I thought about how we had kept Sandy company and fed him scraps, lying with him on the floating door, sitting in the shade of the cove, standing as firmly as we could while what we'd had together crumbled like a sandcastle inside us. I felt sad that we hadn't known ice cream was his favourite thing. We would have given him one if we had.

'We're just a small chapter in Sandy's much bigger story with them,' I said.

'Do you think we lost our warrior battle?' Beth said.

'Sandy won his.'

'And we're licking our wounds.'

'I think we might have to keep fighting inside really hard for another day like this,' I said, aware now that the day would come when Beth would go too.

'Do you have inner-city riots?' Beth said, smiling through her sadness.

Yes, I did.

And while we were deciding about how to say goodbye to Sandy, I asked Beth about that day she'd lost her passport at the quay and where she had been going. She told me that she had been about to catch a ferry.

'I got in a mood with Mum and Dad and felt homesick,' she explained. 'I wanted to go home and be with my friends and other people in our family,' she said. 'I thought that I could catch a ferry and then fly home from the mainland on my own because Mum and Dad said we wouldn't be going home until September. Sometimes it feels like I can't wait any longer.' Beth was full of surprises. We were the same in lots of ways. 'But then I lost my passport.

'It was prickling hot that day and you were there on the quay on your own,' she went on. 'And where the ground was hot I saw you shimmering in the heat haze, as if you were walking on water, and I wondered who you were.' I blinked at her description. 'I wasn't brave enough to go home on my own anyway.'

She'd seen me looking at the ferries, although she didn't know I was looking for Grandfather, and she thought maybe I was someone like her who wanted to go home too. How could she tell all that without even speaking to me?

'I didn't even notice that I'd started thinking of Sandy as belonging to me because I didn't begin with him and I won't end with him. Maybe that means you can feel belonging to someone, or a dog, just for a while,' I said.

'I think you understand me more than most people,' Beth said.

She had a friend called Judy back home. They'd grown up together. Beth said she sent postcards to Judy from wherever she was in the world, and occasionally they phoned each other. But even then Beth felt she could only talk about how beautiful the place was or how the sun was shining, the beaches fine, the sea glorious. It was what tourists did, and yet she didn't feel like a tourist. When she was at home spending time with her friend they talked as they discovered the world together. Instant history, she called it. Something they created together. She missed Judy, having a special person to share things with, without saying a word sometimes. It was like that with me and Grandfather. It was like that with Beth and me too now.

Beth found it hard to make real friends while her parents travelled because most other people were on holiday where she went. But she had made friends with me, swum in the sea with me, and she would leave me behind this time too. There was nothing either of us could do about that. Somehow we knew we had to learn from our experience of letting Sandy go that it was the things that happened in our lives that were like sandcastles. We built something amazing while we were together, and we would always have the memory of that holding us strong inside ourselves, even when the sea took us away from each other on the tide.

Beth and I didn't wave from the quay as the ferry left. But we watched, standing side by side, sharing our sadness and Sandy's joy. Sandy and his owners boarded the ferry home and made themselves comfortable on the deck. Sandy stood up on the bench with his paws on the side and lifted his nose to the wind. He turned to look at us, his long hair blowing freely in the sea breeze as the ferry pulled away. He was going back home, to the place Mr and Mrs Tassi had made for him, where he belonged. The big longing in him was gone now, dissolved. That was all that mattered.

My heart suddenly leaped as something occurred to me. 'Sandy was the sign all along!' I said. And he had turned up as unexpectedly as the pineapples on the beach. 'I don't belong to the cottage, this island or the sea. It's Grandfather that makes me feel I can belong *anywhere*.'

Beth smiled, then laughed. 'It's people, isn't it? That's how we really feel our belonging.'

'Our roots are in our souls! And we take them with us wherever we go! That's what Grandfather would want me to know!'

We didn't have the cottage to return to any more, but it didn't matter now. Part of me had never left Grandfather and part of him had never left me. I felt that, strongly inside myself, how I was anchored to him no matter what happened in my memory, in my history, in our story of two souls that shared a love of the sea.

'Where are we going tomorrow?' Beth said.

There were two islands that I had thought might be where Grandfather was. Saras, island of the fishermen, and Anikonisi, the island of belonging.

But I wasn't sure any more. If Sandy was the sign, but Grandfather hadn't been on Thyra where Sandy came from, then where could he be?

'I don't know yet,' I said. 'But Sandy has to be the key.'

22

Sandy had taught Beth and me so much while he was with us, and because of him we found how to be stronger inside ourselves to meet the challenges of the world we found ourselves in. Sandy had happily lived with us for a while and we would never forget him. Perhaps a part of him had grown roots that would always be attached to our souls. But we learned to be happy that he had his own place with the people he really belonged to. And, more than ever, I knew that the longing I had would only stop when I was with Grandfather again.

Uncle was waiting for me when I got back to the restaurant, Maria at his side. He frowned at my hair, but Maria said how handsome I looked, so he reached out and rubbed at the sides of my head where it was shortest and didn't say anything else about it.

'I want you here for the next few days,' Uncle said. 'We've got the big summer barbecue coming up and you'll have lots of jobs to do.' This was the biggest event of the year for Uncle and he relied on making extra money from it. Hundreds of people would come and dance on the beach, and the biggest fish would be grilled on the barbecues for everyone to share.

'But Beth and I want to go to one of the islands for our final trip,' I said, anxious but trying not to show it.

'I heard the dog's gone home now,' Uncle said, as Maria chewed at her nail. 'So you won't need to go.'

Startled into silence now he knew my excuse for taking the trips had gone, the night insects seemed louder than ever, whirring and buzzing until they were so loud it felt unbearable. But it wasn't Maria who had told Uncle. Mrs Halimeda had seen Beth and me on the quay – just passing, she'd told Uncle – and had seen the dog leave. She'd reported it to Uncle because she was wondering what I was up to, and was I behaving myself after the appalling behaviour she'd witnessed recently outside Grandfather's cottage.

I struggled to find what to say, ashamed at having

been caught out again, when Uncle asked what I'd been doing at the cottage, asking me once more, his voice rising, 'Have I not taken care of you? Have I not been a good uncle to you? Have I not taught you good things?'

Maria tugged at Uncle's arm, saying he wasn't to yell.

'Yes, Uncle,' I said. Somehow, since making myself strong enough to let Sandy go and sharing my feelings with Beth, it now seemed easier to tell him what was true about me. 'You taught me lots of good things, and I know when you yell it's not me making you yell because I know you love me.' Uncle now looked startled. 'You've taught me to care for others, to feed those who are hungry, to share what I have, to look after anyone who needed something from me.'

Uncle's bottom lip trembled. He folded his arms

round himself and Maria slid her hand through his arm to hold on to him too.

'Have I been a good nephew?' I asked him.

His breath caught; he nodded. 'Of course you have, Azi,' Maria said for him, and he nodded again.

Grandfather hadn't told anyone else but me what had happened to his fishing boat. But I knew. It was time Uncle knew too.

'I want to find Grandfather,' I said. 'I love you too, Uncle, but I don't know who I am without him here because sometimes I don't even feel like I belong in my skin and my clothes and my flip-flops. Nobody can make me feel I belong like Grandfather does, the same way Grandfather didn't know who he was without his fishing boat. I need to tell him that too and I need him to come back because otherwise I feel I'm like driftwood washed up on the beach and left behind by the tide.'

Uncle covered his eyes with his hand and Maria looked at him hard.

'He was a fool, taking the boat out while he was drunk,' Uncle said, but there was no heat in his voice, no anger, only something much softer, like pity.

'He wasn't drunk,' I said. 'He didn't start drinking grog until *after* he lost his boat, after the summer beach party two years ago.'

The beach party that Uncle held every summer took a lot of work. Strings of bulbs got propped up along the beach, guiding everyone to Uncle's. Greek dancers, singers and a band for everyone to dance to would go on most of the night while everyone feasted from the ovens. Grandfather was out in his fishing boat earlier that day, watching signs from the sea to get a good catch, something special for Uncle's party.

Grandfather had seen a huge shadow in the water. A prize for Uncle. Grandfather had taken his sea-fishing rod and swung the hook and line and bait far out into the fish's path.

'It was a monster from the deep,' Grandfather had told me afterwards.

'What kind of monster?' I'd said.

'Strong and sleek and shining like silver treasure!' he'd said. 'Taller than you and me put together, Azi. Maybe three or four metres to the tip of the sword at the end of its nose! A mighty, mighty creature!'

The swordfish had taken the bait. Grandfather's feet were wedged against the side of the boat as he leaned back to pull it in, the reel buzzing as the swordfish tugged away, diving deeper and deeper. The line ran out and out, and Grandfather had slowly reeled it back, losing ground again and again when the monster almost took him overboard. The swordfish was so strong it had pulled Grandfather's boat along with it. Patiently, for hours, Grandfather had waited for it to grow weak, reeling it in a little at a time, but all the while the monster was towing Grandfather's boat to some rocks, invisible just below the surface of the water. When the boat hit the rocks Grandfather was knocked from his feet. He lost his rod, the monster and the battle. His boat had sprung a leak and he'd motored to shallower waters before abandoning ship and letting the sea take his boat while he swam ashore.

Grandfather didn't want Uncle to know that he'd let him down, never telling him about the giant swordfish. I remembered Uncle yelling at

Grandfather that night because he had only brought him small fish and not enough for that special occasion. He'd had to send me out, running around everywhere I could think of to make up for what Grandfather hadn't brought back in his net.

'Uncle loves us both but he has to yell sometimes,' Grandfather had said to me after the party was over. 'If all that yelling didn't come out, it would boil and boil up inside him and we wouldn't want him to go *kaboom*, would we, Azi?'

I learned that once in a while monsters were stronger than men.

After I told Uncle the story he put his hands over his face, rubbed his eyes and sighed so deeply I thought he might never start breathing again.

That night was important for Uncle too. Without the extra money that came in, his business would have struggled to survive over the winter. That night was important for all of us.

Uncle looked out towards the sea, and without turning back said, 'I want you to clear the beach first thing in the morning, Azi, and make sure it stays clean. Hand out these flyers too,' he said, which were invitations to the summer barbecue. 'I still need you here.'

23

THE SUMMER BARBECUE CAME AND WENT WITH music and dancing. Beth hung around but Uncle kept me busy. Maria passed a message to me a few days later. Nick had called again and was sorry but he still had no news about Grandfather.

'He also said he'd been taking a look at a possible building plot and had met some people from the Turtle-Conservation Society, who have opposed his plans to build,' Maria said. 'They knew you, Azi. What was that all about?'

'We met them on Chelona,' I said. 'They want to keep people away from the turtle nesting site there, so Nick wouldn't be able to build a hotel near it.'

Maria shrugged. 'Small world,' she said. 'But sorry there's no good news.'

And then Uncle at last said I could take the day off. I wouldn't tell him but I was still going to look for Grandfather. But to which island were Beth and I going to go? I decided I would have to tell her everything and then maybe she could help me work it out.

'That was the only time Grandfather didn't triumph over a monster of the sea,' I explained to her as I finished my story.

'Maybe he's gone to find it and finish his battle,'

Beth said, her eyes glistening, her shoulder pressed against mine.

We thought and thought, making a list of the islands, crossing off those that didn't seem to have any signs to suggest that Grandfather might have gone there. We started again. What were the signs? Where did they lead us? The passport had led me to Beth. The door had led both of us to Thyra where we found Sandy's home.

'What about the turtle?' Beth said.

'We know he's not on Chelona,' I said. 'Andreas would have said.'

'You said Sandy was the sign,' Beth said, scratching her head. 'Perhaps he really is the sign in other ways, not just finding out where your sense of belonging is.'

We thought and thought but all the islands had sandy beaches.

'And there isn't a Fílos island . . .' I jumped up and slapped my hands over my head. 'But there is a dog island!'

'You've found it, haven't you?' Beth laughed.

'Skylos!' I shouted. 'It's Skylos. It's an island shaped like a dog and it's really close by. And you're right, Beth. It was near Skylos that Grandfather caught the silver monster fish!'

He had to be there.

Skylos was the only place I wanted to go. I told Maria but not Uncle. Beth told her parents she wanted to go anyway and they were fine with that.

We caught the ferry but it wasn't the same without Sandy. Not having to give him a space to sit between us at the front, we moved closer to each other. We missed his wispy fur tickling us when he put his head on the railings as we leaned on our arms at the front of the boat. We missed his quiet company, and his patience and softness and gracefulness and golden hair. But we found many more things to talk about and shared stories of our time with him and they became great tales, overlapping but never fully told.

'The more time we spend together, the harder it's going to be when you go,' I told Beth.

'Do you mean you'd rather not spend time with me?' Beth said.

'No!' I said straight away. 'I mean . . . you know.'

She smiled. 'My dad says that just because something's hard to do, it doesn't mean you shouldn't do it. In fact, he said the hardest things always turn out to teach you the best things in the end.'

Beth hadn't bought any souvenirs. They took up too much room on her parents' sailing boat. She liked to travel light.

'Would you like this?' I said. I gave her a passport

photo of me and Sandy. I wanted her to have it. 'It's small and thin so it won't take up too much space.'

'You'd be surprised,' she said, laughing, but I was confused. 'You and a beautiful, gentle dog have already taken up masses of room in my memory, but the more room you take up, the more I seem to have.'

It sounded good. 'It's like a vision at first,' I said, because it was the same for me. 'Then you start to feel you can build something from the people you have history with, like the foundations of a house, and then after a little while you start to feel as if you have made a good strong place inside yourself.'

'Yes,' she said. 'And I learned that from you.'

As we approached the dock at Skylos my heart felt like it was going to burst. At the quayside, some of the older men sipping thick black coffee at the tavernas had known Grandfather a long time ago when he was raising Uncle, when they were all much younger men. Soon they dived into their memories, recalling Uncle as a teenager too and how the life of a fisherman hadn't suited him when he'd worked alongside Grandfather for a while. They said that Grandfather hadn't been disappointed that Uncle didn't follow in his footsteps. Evander was a man of the sea; he knew how to be alone out on the water. Some of the old men had been fishermen too, and remembered enjoying the quietness of their working lives when the emptiness of the sea released them from everyday worries. They got sentimental about how they had found their happiness with whatever came their way through the water. They drew me in with all their talk that was almost as familiar as Grandfather's and left me starving for

Grandfather's stories again when their memories dried up and they said they wouldn't expect to see Evander on Skylos.

Emptiness filled me. Every time I built something inside me, it collapsed like a sandcastle.

Beth said she thought I might want to be on my own, but she was around, if I wanted to find her. I asked her to stay. And while we were sitting quietly in the cove something unexpected happened.

The message in a bottle that I had thrown out to sea came bobbing and rolling in on a wave and washed up on the shore. The thing is I knew that when I'd thrown it out that the current would take it clockwise on the sea, and that it would eventually land on one of the islands, although I couldn't be sure which. It would end up *somewhere*! But the only way it could have landed on this shore was if someone knew where to throw it back in the sea for the tide to bring it here again. Was it another sign from the sea? Had Grandfather found it? Was I hoping too much?

I ran down to the shoreline and picked it up. The photos of me and the passport application were still inside. But nothing else. Had Grandfather thrown it back in the sea to tell me not to come and find him?

'I don't know what it means,' I said.

'I've been thinking about all the signs from the sea,' Beth said. 'And the funny thing is that the turtle, the door, Sandy and this bottle all came to the same place. All the signs ended up *here*.'

'Does it mean I have to stay here, with Uncle, for good?' I said.

'It might not be that,' Beth said, but I could tell that she was as disappointed as me. We'd both have to think about what it all meant and about what I should do next, and when Beth left and I went back to the restaurant Uncle was waiting for me again.

'A courier called with a parcel for you today,' Uncle said, handing me a brown padded envelope. The sender's address was printed at the top. It was from Papadopoulos Property Developers.

I wasn't expecting Nick to send me anything, but maybe it was some information about Grandfather. I ripped the package open, desperate to see. There were large sheets of thick paper, folded smaller over and over, but I couldn't make out what I was looking at and then Uncle took it from me.

'What is all this?' he said. 'Building plans?'

Maria had joined us and was looking over his shoulder.

They were plans to build a house so someone could live permanently near the turtle nesting site.

'Why has he sent this to me?' I said.

Uncle slammed down the papers. 'You're not going to live near the nesting site on Chelona, Azi!' He blew up like a pufferfish. 'Not with Grandfather, not with anyone! You're staying here, with me! I promised I would take care of you!'

Maria pulled the papers from his hands.

'The plans are for the Turtle-Conservation Society and it's not for Chelona,' Maria said, raising her voice.

It was for here, at the cove.

Maria put her hands on her hips. 'And I've just about heard enough of your yelling for once,' she said firmly to Uncle. 'We all have!'

Uncle blinked at Maria and was about to open his mouth. She put a finger to his lips. 'Shush,' she said. 'You say you love this boy, and I know you do, and I know you try to take care of him, but Lord knows it's not exactly a bundle of fun around here for any of us sometimes. How about you prove to Azi that you want him here?'

I knew Uncle wanted me there. I knew deep down he cared very much for me, and that we also belonged to each other in some way, but apart from that I didn't know what Maria meant.

'Go on, tell him,' she said to Uncle. 'I've watched that boy grow under . . . difficult circumstances, and I know he will understand if you tell him what both of you should have told him a long time ago.' She pulled up some chairs and told us to sit down. I'd never seen Uncle be bossed about by anyone else before.

'Uncle has something he needs very much to tell you,' Maria said, and then she went out the back in the kitchen, no doubt listening for any yelling.

Uncle sighed and rubbed at the short hair at the side of my head.

'You know Grandfather used to tell you stories about creatures from the sea?'

I nodded, the familiar feeling putting me at ease.

'I've got a story too, about another kind of monster.'

24

'THERE WERE TWO WARS,' UNCLE BEGAN. 'WHEN Grandfather was a young man he left the country where he had been raised to come and live here, on this island. But his roots were still in the country he had come from, where he grew as a boy.'

Uncle told me that Grandfather hadn't left his home country because he was unhappy there or because anything had been wrong, but simply because he'd always loved the sea, and as a young man he'd found his heart's content, here on the island surrounded by the sea. He visited his home country whenever he wanted: his family, his friends, the places he loved. But the warm currents always carried him back here.

'And then a war came to his homeland.' Uncle dabbed at the corners of his eyes as the story spilled out. He cried over rooftops fallen to the ground, homes shattered and splintered, families fractured; Uncle's heritage and part of his history too, destroyed by monsters. Places of worship were stripped of dignity. The shining colour of spirit sucked from the walls, from all the people, clouded with the dust of destruction. Tears quietly washed Uncle's cheeks.

Whole cities of houses had been broken and people were homeless. Some of them escaped across the land, some across the sea, but many fell with the ruins. The walls of the city hadn't kept people apart from each other, but once the walls were torn down there was nothing to keep them together. When war destroyed cities it also destroyed its people. Grandfather could never go back to his original home, even if he wanted to.

The second war came. Between Grandfather and the grog.

Unable to go home, hearing no news of relatives lost, he found some measure of memory and comfort with the spirits in the bottle of alcohol.

'This was all before you . . . just before you were born, Azi,' Uncle said.

He described what the drink did to Grandfather, making him look like wreckage, yellow-skinned and haggard, soggy with drink but dried out to the brittle bone. Grandfather had been safe, here on the island, but others fled his home country. There was no news of anyone he knew, but he lived in hope that his relatives and friends, even his neighbours had fled safely. Some took a boat across the sea, and on a flimsy raft left for an unpromised land.

The unsteady boat overflowed with people.

Water poured in as their souls cried out, and they were lost to the arms of the waves.

Grandfather had been out in his fishing boat.

'There was no birth certificate, nothing to say where you came from,' Uncle said quietly, his voice cracking. 'You were born before the sea took who you belonged to.' His chest heaved. 'Grandfather found you, Azi: a baby wrapped in a life jacket, floating on flotsam in the sea.'

'Me?' I said, adrift, unsteady, not really knowing

how I belonged in this story, and yet understanding that this was my history.

'You came from the sea, Azi,' Uncle said. 'Isn't that what Grandfather told you?'

I was born at sea? Did it make me what I was? Sea boy, aqua boy, a creature from the sea? Did being born at sea make me who I am?

Or . . .

Was I made from the old man who saved me from the sea?

While Uncle told me what had happened next, I felt how real it was, right inside and all through me, as if the story was the salt in the water of life inside my body. As if it was true history and my own memory.

It was Grandfather I gazed up at from the water as a baby. The sun in my sky.

The war Uncle spoke of had begun before I was

born, but it was still raging, destroying, hurting now. But in that story were moments that reminded me of when I stood on the edge of the land and the edge of the sea, when I dived in under the water, when I looked up and saw Grandfather looking down, his strong hairy arms reaching to pull me out.

Grandfather had given me shelter and taken me in as his own.

'He didn't touch a drop of grog after he found you,' Uncle finished. 'He had no need. You were . . . you *are* his everything: his family, his country, his home, something that's very hard to explain, but . . .'

'But where you feel you belong,' I said.

'Yes, that's what he always said. Your life was worth more than all the buildings that were lost. You were the sign from the sea that he could fight the battle inside to save something of himself. For you.'

Uncle had agreed that Grandfather should raise me; the alternative – handing me in to the authorities as a refugee – was far less secure than what he felt he could offer me. 'The boy will need people who will understand him,' Grandfather had said. 'He has no homeland, no family, and he will need to feel some sense of belonging. I will give him that.'

But Uncle had warned Grandfather that if he ever touched a drop of grog again, Uncle would take me from him and raise me instead.

When Grandfather lost his boat it made him weak again. Uncle saw that now – it had made Grandfather tip the bottle to his lips again. The grog called, offering mirages, dredging up memories of the past – the war and everything that had been lost. His days were filled with sea monsters he could not beat. He was lost, sinking like a shipwreck. Uncle took me in instead.

'Did you tell Grandfather to leave?' I asked Uncle, hoping with everything I had that the answer was no, that Uncle only fulfilled his part of the promise to make sure I was raised well.

'I didn't tell him to leave,' he said. 'But Grandfather knew he had to go. He told me before he left about you taking the bottle from him and the broken glass and how he couldn't bear that he had caused you any hurt and that he was the monster and a danger to you. He left so he could keep you safe. He wouldn't have wanted to offer you less than all of himself, all of his history, all of his love of the sea. You were the pearl he found there. He left of his own accord, Azi. He knew I would look after you.'

'I would rather have Grandfather and the grog any day over not having him at all,' I said, feeling the sadness of missing him overwhelm me again.

'Yes, and he knew that too. That's why he couldn't stay.'

'I want to find him, Uncle.'

Uncle sighed, said he hoped I'd understand what he had to tell me next. He said a small story would help me see the bigger story.

'The grog is like . . . like a monster octopus.'

'Or a giant swordfish?' I said.

'Yes, just like the one you told me about. It dragged Grandfather down with it and wouldn't let him go, and he can't let go either.'

'But he's fighting a battle with it, isn't he?' I said.

Uncle nodded. 'If he can defeat the monster, he'll come back. Until then we have to leave him be while the battle goes on. Only he can do it, Azi.'

'He's a warrior deep inside, Uncle,' I said. 'He will win.'

'Yes, I hope he will too.'

Together, Grandfather and I were a home to each other. We were our own walls to keep each other safe. We shared one heart and life. Grandfather had to end his war before he could come home by himself. No matter how much I searched for Grandfather it wouldn't have brought him back.

But he'd come across the sea. I still knew he would.

25

GRANDFATHER HAD TAUGHT ME TO BE PATIENT, and it was a battle that I wanted to win, knowing he was fighting for us somewhere too. The rest of the summer I stopped looking for signs. Beth was my constant companion. Now we knew so much about each other on the inside, we could enjoy and make our own history together for a while. The closer it got to the time she had to go home and we'd be apart, the more inseparable we felt.

Nick's company worked on building a turtle-watch station and I saw it turn from a vision to a plan and something real. They built the hut on the edge of the sea and the edge of the land, on the rocks at the cove, at the place I first saw Sandy. And then, one day at the end of the summer, Nick came to show me around now it was completed.

The building was supported by stilts over the rocks and sunk into the seabed. It had a bathroom with a bath between two bedrooms, and one big room for cooking and eating and sitting and watching, with wide glass windows with a view of the whole cove and the sea. From the blue door at the side, a long steady path led down to the beach.

'What do you think?' Nick said.

'It's good,' I said. 'I thought it was going to be like a kiosk but it's more like a home.'

He laughed. 'I designed it from what you told me about you and your grandfather. Now we just need someone who would be willing to live in it and spend their days watching the sea and the cove to protect the turtles.'

I looked up at him and he nodded and it was already there in my heart who he meant.

'I couldn't tell you before, because he wasn't quite ready, but your Grandfather funded this project from selling his cottage. He asked me to build this house. It's for you and him,' he said. 'Time is a great healer, Azi.'

Today was the extraordinary day I had waited two years and three months for. The signs from the sea hadn't meant what I'd thought. The turtle might have meant that in time Grandfather would win his battle, in his own time. The door might have shown me it didn't matter where I lived, that his house was not the place where I belonged. *He* was, because he was the one that gave me the feeling of belonging. The passport wasn't a sign for me to go anywhere, but I was lucky it led me to find Beth. The thing was, all the signs came here. *Here*, to me. But it was Sandy who had given me so much. He showed me that I had to let go completely of searching, because then . . .

'He's coming across the sea, isn't he?' I said.

Nick looked at his watch. 'He's on his way on the ferry now.'

It was a Monday, and all I wanted was for it to be the most ordinary day for me ever.

* * *

I took the path down to the cove, now fenced off at either end to protect the turtle nest. It would always be mine and Grandfather's, though. I stood and gazed at what I'd see every morning, every day, every night. The sea was calm, as if all the restlessness had gone from it.

I sat by the old door with a new tin bucket and stared into it until a shadow fell across me. The sand was hot and I moved over and he came and sat down. I brushed the hairs on his arm, to see the tattoo. The tentacles of the sea monster seemed faint against the strong blue anchor. He rubbed at my knee, at the scar left from the glass.

'It wasn't your fault, Azi,' he said. 'You're safe now. There'll be no more grog.'

He leaned over to see inside the bucket, but it was empty, and he just nodded and smiled because we knew each other so well, and he would know that I had no need to stare into a small, separated sea world now he was back and moored alongside me.

'I came from the sea,' I said.

'Washed into my arms like a miracle,' he said.

I peeled the foil from the plates Uncle had given me, offered him a cold drink of water, which he took, sipped, smacked his lips and smiled. We ate grilled fish and salad, then I passed him a spoon and a jar of honey.

'Did I ever tell you about the monster octopus?' he said, dipping in the spoon, filling it and passing it to me. 'It had ten, maybe twelve arms, thick as a man's chest . . .'

We shared sea-monster stories, our histories of battles and wars won and our triumph. We watched while the quiet sea rolled against the sand, washed the shore clean that we had sat upon time and time again. We had already built a new place inside us from the ruins of the past. The years apart dissolved away with the last of the burning sun melting into the horizon, and the moon rose. We didn't need anything else. In the silence we were as full and boundless as the sea, deeper than the Mariana Trench.

And then something flickered in the sand. A tiny turtle pushed itself out of the nest. And, before long, hundreds of tiny turtles were flipping across the sand to the glossy marble path of the moon on the sea, and into the dancing waves. There were nests everywhere. The turtle hadn't been alone all along.

I stood up, reached out and clenched Grandfather's hand in mine, pulling him up. 'Let's see the new place you have built to go around us, where we can make new roots.'

'Even plants can be transplanted,' he said.

'And we are two of a kind.'

An old fisherman and the boy from the sea.

26

GRANDFATHER SITS AT THE COVE. HE WAS A fisherman so he knows how to be alone with the sea. And when I am there with him we know the boundless reach of all the seas and it feels like it's where we have always belonged, that we were always here.

Beth left the following week and I jumped high, waving and watching until long after their sailing boat disappeared over the horizon. Since Grandfather had come back she was waiting patiently for her time to return home, knowing it would be everything to her. Sandy and I had taught her that.

A week later, the post-office service had tried to deliver a parcel to me, but Grandfather and I had been down at the cove and they'd left a card to say I had to collect it.

'I know who you are and where you come from and where you live,' Mrs Halimeda said impatiently as I handed her the card. It was hard facing someone who still thought of me like that, but I had learned that people could say what they liked about me, about Grandfather, or tell me I didn't belong here, because the only ones who matter are those who tell you that you do.

'No, you don't know who I am or who my

grandfather is,' I said. 'You only know our name and address.'

Beth had sent me a handful of sand.

It might seem to you that all of us in this story were there at the beginning and there at the end. But my story wasn't the beginning or the end. We are all part of a much bigger story, of monsters and wars, of brave hearts and warriors and triumph, of belonging to each other, but one day some of us met, and it was only while we were together that we could see we needed each other for the battles we had to face. We didn't even know that we belonged to the same story until we met, and we had no idea how we belonged until we fought alongside each other. With Beth, the countries where we lived were separated by the sea, but we are all still joined together in a history that belongs to all of us. The time we spend together is like building a sandcastle on the beach. And every time the sea comes in to wash it all away we build it up again and again.

Acknowledgements

When this story finally came to light, it became a fishing expedition to reel in something from under the surface, and I'm surprised at what rose up from the deep. Thank you to my dad who took my sister and I to a Greek island many years ago, where we stayed in a house next to the beach and heard the sea from our bedroom windows. Thank you to my brother-in-law, Rupert, who talked to me about his encounters with turtles and, perhaps unwittingly, revealed the sense of a man who belongs on the sea. There were also some who contributed in conversation to the story and I hope I have told them all as it happened how it was appreciated.

As always, my thanks are to those whose words encourage and support the writer, the writing and the heart of this story, especially Rachel Denwood, Michelle Misra, Samantha Stewart, Lowri Ribbons and all at HarperCollins who have had a hand in putting it all together, Julia Churchill, and my family.

Cally saw her mum, bright and real and
alive. But no one believes her, so Cally's
stopped talking. Now a mysterious grey
wolfhound has started following her
everywhere. Perhaps he knows that Cally
was telling the truth . . .

Leo dreams about being a hero. In his imagination he is a fearsome gladiator, but he wants to be a hero in real life.

Then the boys at school dare Leo to do something he knows is wrong and he lets everybody down. How can he make things right again?

When a little dog called Jack Pepper goes missing it will take a true hero to find him and bring him home . . .

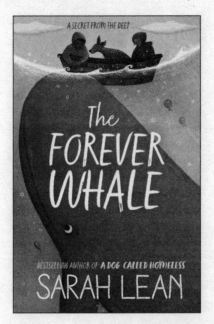

Hannah's grandad loves telling stories from his past, but there's one that he can't remember . . . one that Hannah knows is important.

When a whale appears off the coast, clues to Grandad's secret begin to surface. Hannah is determined to solve the mystery, but as she gets closer to the truth she finds Grandad's story is more extraordinary than she ever imagined.